THE TRAIL TO SEVEN PINES

A HOPALONG CASSIDY NOVEL

**Bantam Books by Louis L'Amour
Ask your bookseller for the books you
have missed.**

NOVELS

BENDIGO SHAFTER
BORDEN CHANTRY
BRIONNE
THE BROKEN GUN
THE BURNING HILLS
THE CALIFORNIOS
CALLAGHEN
CATLOW
CHANCY
THE CHEROKEE TRAIL
COMSTOCK LODE
CONAGHER
CROSSFIRE TRAIL
DARK CANYON
DOWN THE LONG HILLS
THE EMPTY LAND
FAIR BLOWS THE WIND
FALLON
THE FERGUSON RIFLE
THE FIRST FAST DRAW
FLINT
GUNS OF THE
   TIMBERLANDS
HANGING WOMAN CREEK
THE HAUNTED MESA
HELLER WITH A GUN
THE HIGH GRADERS
HIGH LONESOME
HONDO
HOW THE WEST WAS WON
THE IRON MARSHAL
THE KEY-LOCK MAN
KID RODELO
KILKENNY

KILLOE
KILRONE
KIOWA TRAIL
LAST OF THE BREED
LAST STAND AT PAPAGO
   WELLS
THE LONESOME GODS
THE MAN CALLED NOON
THE MAN FROM
   SKIBBEREEN
THE MAN FROM THE
   BROKEN HILLS
MATAGORDA
MILO TALON
THE MOUNTAIN VALLEY
   WAR
NORTH TO THE RAILS
OVER ON THE DRY SIDE
PASSIN' THROUGH
THE PROVING TRAIL
THE QUICK AND THE DEAD
RADIGAN
REILLY'S LUCK
THE RIDER OF LOST CREEK
RIVERS WEST
THE SHADOW RIDERS
SHALAKO
SHOWDOWN AT YELLOW
   BUTTE
SILVER CANYON
SITKA
SON OF A WANTED MAN
TAGGART
THE TALL STRANGER
TO TAME A LAND

TUCKER
UNDER THE SWEETWATER
  RIM
UTAH BLAINE
THE WALKING DRUM
WESTWARD THE TIDE
WHERE THE LONG GRASS
  BLOWS

SHORT STORY COLLECTIONS

BOWDRIE
BOWDRIE'S LAW
BUCKSKIN RUN
DUTCHMAN'S FLAT
THE HILLS OF HOMICIDE
LAW OF THE DESERT
  BORN
LONG RIDE HOME
LONIGAN
NIGHT OVER THE
  SOLOMONS
THE OUTLAWS OF
  MESQUITE
THE RIDER OF THE RUBY
  HILLS
RIDING FOR THE BRAND
THE STRONG SHALL LIVE
THE TRAIL TO CRAZY MAN
WAR PARTY
WEST FROM SINGAPORE
YONDERING

SACKETT TITLES

SACKETT'S LAND
TO THE FAR BLUE
  MOUNTAINS
THE WARRIOR'S PATH
JUBAL SACKETT
RIDE THE RIVER
THE DAYBREAKERS
SACKETT
LANDO
MOJAVE CROSSING
MUSTANG MAN
THE LONELY MEN
GALLOWAY
TREASURE MOUNTAIN
LONELY ON THE
  MOUNTAIN
RIDE THE DARK TRAIL
THE SACKETT BRAND
THE SKY-LINERS

THE HOPALONG CASSIDY NOVELS

THE RUSTLERS OF WEST
  FORK
THE TRAIL TO SEVEN
  PINES

NONFICTION

EDUCATION OF A
  WANDERING MAN
FRONTIER
THE SACKETT
  COMPANION:
  A Personal Guide to the
  Sackett Novels
A TRAIL OF MEMORIES:
  The Quotations of Louis
  L'Amour, compiled by
  Angelique L'Amour

POETRY

SMOKE FROM THIS ALTAR

LOUIS L'AMOUR

THE
TRAIL TO
SEVEN PINES

A HOPALONG CASSIDY NOVEL

BANTAM BOOKS
NEW YORK · TORONTO · LONDON · SYDNEY · AUCKLAND
A Bantam Large Print Edition

THE TRAIL TO SEVEN PINES
A Bantam Book

Publishing History
Bantam hardcover edition published June 1992
Bantam large print edition / July 1992

Previously published as Hopalong Cassidy and the Trail to Seven Pines
by Louis L'Amour (writing as Tex Burns).

ISBN 0-385-42369-1

Published simultaneously in the United States and Canada

Bantam Books are published by Bantam Books, a division of Bantam Doubleday Dell Publishing
Group, Inc. Its trademark, consisting of the words "Bantam Books" and the portrayal of a rooster,
is Registered in U.S. Patent and Trademark Office and in other countries. Marca Registrada.
Bantam Books, 666 Fifth Avenue, New York, New York 10103.

PRINTED IN THE UNITED STATES OF AMERICA

RRH 0 9 8 7 6 5 4 3 2 1

**This Large Print Book carries the
Seal of Approval of N.A.V.H.**

THE TRAIL TO SEVEN PINES

A HOPALONG CASSIDY NOVEL

CHAPTER 1

TWO DEAD MEN

Hopalong Cassidy stopped his white gelding on the bald backbone of the ridge. No soil covered the wind-swept sandstone, only a few gnarled cedars that seemed, as is their way, to draw nourishment from the very rock itself. In this last hour before sunset the air was of startling clarity, so much so that objects upon the mountainside across the valley stood out, clearly defined as though but a few yards away instead of as many miles.

Where he sat the sun was bright, but in the west, which was his direction, towering masses of cumulus piled to majestic heights, dwarfing the mountains to insignificance. The crests of the mighty clouds were glorious with sunlight, but the flat undersides were sullen with impending rain. Hopalong squinted appraisingly at the sky and became no happier at what he saw.

Seven Pines, proudly claiming title as the toughest town west of anywhere, was a good twelve miles off, hidden in the mountains across the valley. Long before he could ride a third of that distance those clouds would be giving the valley a thorough drenching. What he needed now was shelter, and he needed it badly.

So it was that he sat in his saddle studying the country with careful eyes. The stage route was but a mile or so to the north, but he had heard of no shelter there and so far his information had been most accurate. Even as he watched, the gigantic cloud moved nearer, lightning stabbed through it, and the thunder rolled and grumbled.

To the south and west the valley narrowed before spewing out into the vast waste of Adobe Flat. Waterless most of the time, after a rain it would become a slippery, greasy surface that concealed unexpected sinks and mud traps. Close by, the mountainside was broken and serrated, carved by upheaval and erosion. There were notches among the rocks in some of the canyons, but they might well prove deathtraps in such a storm as this would be. Hopalong Cassidy had lived too long in the

West not to realize the danger that lay in the bottoms of canyons and dry washes. It was such a sudden rush of water that had finally ended his feud with Tex Ewalt and brought them together as friends, but more often than not, it meant only death to the unwary traveler.

Suddenly, as he was about to ride on, a movement caught his eye and he drew up sharply. From the mouth of a canyon below and to the southwest a small group of riders had emerged. Something in their bunched way of riding warned Cassidy, and he kneed his mount to the partial concealment of a juniper. At this distance even his field glasses offered him no marks of identification, save a single white splotch on the flank of one horse and that same horse's white nose. There were six riders, and they moved north at a rapid pace, keeping close to the mountain and choosing a route that offered cover from view.

He watched them until they disappeared, scowling slightly, for he knew this land in which he lived. Although a stranger in this area, he was far from strange to the West and western ways, and it seemed these men were riding on a mission. A mission that demanded they remain hidden from anyone passing down the stage-coach road.

"All right, Topper," Hopalong said quietly

to the short-coupled gelding, "let's ride along and see what happens. It's a cinch they know where there's shelter. They won't like to get wet any more than we do."

The white horse moved along, choosing its own trail, heading down and northward on a slant. With another appraising glance at the cloud, much nearer now, Hopalong Cassidy drew his six-shooters one after the other and carefully wiped them free of dust. They were worn silver-plated Colt .45's, their bone handles networked with tiny cracks, their balance perfect. It had been weeks since he had drawn a gun for any reason, but he knew that the price of safety was unresting vigilance.

Seven Pines was his immediate destination, but actually he was just roving across the country. Somewhere to the north, an old friend of the cattle trails, Gibson of the old 3 T L, had a ranch where he lived with his widowed daughter. Hopalong planned to stop with them for a few days before swinging northeast into Montana.

The presence of the riders, even while it promised the proximity of shelter, disturbed him. He had no desire to walk into a range war or any trouble whatsoever. This ride of his was strictly a sightseeing trip, taken with money in his pocket and no feeling of hurry.

A few spattering drops of rain struck his hat brim, sweeping it with a hasty barrage. Hopalong frowned and dug for his slicker, donning it without slowing his pace. By now he was off the ridge and well into a stand of cedar, his eyes busy searching for shelter. Once he glimpsed an old mine dump, but the tunnel was long since caved in and the buildings had collapsed.

When he reached the vague trail skirting the foot of the mountain he found the tracks of the bunch ahead of him. He studied the tracks briefly, reading them as easily as another man might read a page of print. These were fresh horses, well shod, but one horse had the hoof trimmed too narrow, causing him to toe in somewhat. Another dash of rain came, gained impetus, and then proceeded in a downpour that drew a gray veil across the desert and mountains. The sky darkened and the rolling clouds closed out the sun, shutting down all the miles before him with darkness and slashing rain.

The gray streak of a trail led downward from the mine dump, offering a chance of speed, so he lifted the gelding into a canter and went down the mountain to the main road. Halting briefly, he again found the tracks of the riders. Not yet wiped out by the rain, they crossed the road and then ran along through the brush parallel to it.

The shower eased, and Hopalong smelled the old familiar odor that raindrops bring to long-dry dust. Then there was a crash of thunder and more rain, and behind the rain a roaring weight of wind. Now the darkness became absolute, without a chink of light anywhere except for the constant play of lightning. The wide valley was filled with sound, and the rain came down in solid sheets of water turned into a scythe driven by the fierce wind.

He turned onto the stage road, and Topper held to his canter. Then suddenly the storm lulled, and down this hallway of silence Hopalong heard the sudden crash of shots!

Two . . . three more, a light volley . . . and then one. The last was a lone, final shot. The ending of something.

Reining in, Hopalong strained his ears against the sudden silence, listening. There was nothing, and then the rain came again, whispering at first, then mounting in crescendo to new heights of fury. Pushing on, his hat brim pulled low, his slicker collar high around his ears, he wondered at the shots. A cold drop fell down the back of his neck and found a trail down his spine. He shivered and strained his eyes into the blackness ahead.

Riding suddenly onto the scene of a shooting was anything but smart, but this was new
country to him, known only by hearsay, and if
he got off the trail now he could easily wander
out into the valley and become lost. Suddenly
Hopalong felt the gelding's muscles tense and
in a flash of lightning he saw its head come up
sharply. At the same time Hopalong saw, on
the trail ahead, a dark shape sprawled in the
mud!

Drawing up, he waited for lightning. It
came, and he stared beyond the man's body,
but the trail was empty as far as he could see.
Whatever had happened here was now over.
Swinging down beside the fallen man, he
turned him over. Rain splashed on a white,
dead face and over a bullet-riddled body. One
hole was in the head. Shielding a struck match,
Hopalong's lips compressed. This man had
been downed by the other shots, but the last
one had been fired by a gun held against his
skull, burning with its muzzle blast the hair and
skin. Of this man they had made sure.

Quickly he went through the man's pockets, removing his wallet, papers, and what loose
money he could find. These things should go to
the man's relatives, if any, and would help
serve as identification. In this rain they would

soon become soaked and illegible unless protected.

The dead man had made a try for his life. His pistol was gripped in his hand and one shot had been fired.

Standing over him, oblivious of the rain, Hopalong studied the situation. The man had been removed from the stage, for he lay to one side of the trail, and it looked as if he had been given his chance, had taken it, and lost. Cut deeply into the trail were the tracks of the stage. "Holdup," Hoppy muttered. "This hombre either asked for a scrap or had it forced on him. One thing, he doesn't size up like any pilgrim. He'd been to the wars before."

Mounting, Hopalong rode up the trail a short distance, then stopped as a flash of lightning revealed yet another body. Swinging down, Hopalong bent to touch the man, and he groaned. Straightening up, Hopalong waited for another flash of light, then spotted a slight overhang in the rock of the cliff, an overhang that gave promise of growing deeper as the rock curved away from the trail.

Tying his horse to a juniper, Hopalong returned and picked the man up, carrying him deep into the sheltered cleft where no rain fell and where the sand was dry. Gathering dried sticks from the remains of a long-dead tree, he built a fire. When it was burning briskly he put some water on and opened the wounded man's coat and vest. A glance showed the man was hard hit.

The first hole was a flesh wound, low down on the left side. It had bled profusely, and the whole side of the fellow's clothing was soaked with blood. Higher, there was yet another and more serious wound. This one was just over the heart, and Hopalong felt his skin tighten at the look of it.

When the water was hot he took his time bathing the wounds, then bandaged them tightly with a compress made of split and slightly roasted prickly-pear leaves. It was a remedy he had seen Indians and old-timers use for the removal of inflammation and he had nothing else at hand. Familiar as he was with bullet wounds, he knew the man's chance of survival was small, yet the fellow was young, powerfully built, and obviously in excellent health.

Going back for more fuel, Hopalong led his white horse more deeply into the cut and stripped off the saddle. There was a bank of blown-up earth that had sprouted grass, and the gelding was quickly at home. Walking back, Hopalong saw that his patient's eyes were open. The man was staring around him with uncomprehending wonder. Moving closer, Hopalong advised quietly, "Just take it easy, partner. You caught a couple of bad ones."

The man stared at him, his brow puckering. "Who—who are you?"

"Driftin' through. Heard some shootin' ahead of me, and when I came up I found a dead man, and then you."

"Then I nailed one of 'em?"

"Doubt it. This hombre wore a frock coat and a gray hat. Hard-lookin', with a reddish mustache."

"Oh. He was a passenger." The man was quiet for a minute and his breathing was heavy. He was a clean-cut, rather handsome young man with cow country written all over him. He wore two guns and looked like a man who could use them.

"What happened?" Hopalong asked.

"Stickup. I was ridin'—ridin' shotgun. They shot me first off but I stuck it out and figured I nailed one of 'em. Then they got me again and I fell off the stage. They were masked—like always."

"Always?"

"Fourth time in three months . . . This was my first trip. The other guards got it too." A faint smile flickered across the wounded man's face. "Whoever pulls these jobs doesn't like shotgun messengers."

Hopalong had put some broth, made from jerky and a handful of flour, on the fire. It was hot now, and he fed a little to the wounded man. He took his time, letting the man have plenty of time to breathe, hoping the broth would give him added strength. He seemed to have lost a lot of blood.

"What's your name, amigo? I'd better know."

The young fellow stared at him. "That bad? Well, I'm Jesse Lock. Don't reckon anybody will miss me much. You might hunt up my brother and let him know. He's got him a place up in the Roberts Mountains. Name of Ben Lock."

The rain slowed until all that could be heard of it was a trickle of runoff and the slow dripping of the trees. Thankfully, the wounded man settled into a fitful sleep, but his ragged breathing had Hopalong worried. If the stage had made it to Seven Pines there should be a party sent out to look for the men downed in the robbery. But they might believe both men were dead, or that the trail was washed out. Hoppy went back and cinched up the saddle on Topper. He was afraid he would have to leave

Jesse Lock and go for help, instead of waiting
for it to come to them.

The sky was growing gray when Jesse Lock
next opened his eyes, and the first thing he noticed was the saddle on the white horse. His
eyes flickered to Hopalong. "I'm not makin'
out so good," he whispered hoarsely. "Reckon
I'm bad off."

"Yeah." Cassidy eased the wounded man
into a more comfortable position. "How far is
it to Seven Pines? You need a doctor."

"Twelve miles. Find Doc Marsh—he's a
good man."

Hopalong bathed the wounds once more,
and they looked better than he would have expected. He renewed the poultice of prickly
pear, and Lock watched him curiously. "Heard
of that. Indian remedy, ain't it?"

"Yes. I'm goin' for the doc. You'll be all
right?"

The wounded man's eyes were ironically
amused. "Don't reckon I'll wander off and get
a leg broken. And I'm sure not goin' to get any
better without a doctor." He hesitated, looked
at Hopalong almost wistfully, and said slowly,
"Sure do hate to see you go, amigo."

Drawing one of the wounded man's guns,
Hopalong handed it to him. "Just in case," he

said. "They might figure you knew something and come back." He drew the belts nearer. "But I doubt it. I figure you'll be all right."

He headed down the trail at a fast clip, and Topper liked it. He was a horse that always liked to run, and he ran now. Yet they had gone no more than four miles when Hopalong saw a black blotch on the trail ahead that speedily developed into a racing buckboard and a half-dozen riders. There were two men in the buck-board, a blocky man with auburn hair and mustache, and a taller, younger man with a mustache of clipped blond hair and cool but friendly blue eyes. They drew up at Hopalong's lifted hand.

"Wounded man up ahead," he said. "Let's hurry. Is Doc Marsh here?"

The blond young man nodded. "I'm Dr. Marsh."

Hopalong wheeled his horse and led them back up the badly washed trail. One of the men wore a star. He was a tall old man with cold gray eyes and a handlebar mustache. "Who's alive?"

"Lock, he said his name was."

"Talk any?"

Hopalong was acutely conscious that the others were closing around, listening intently.

"He's badly hurt." Hopalong avoided the question. "They get anything?"

"They got it all!" The burly man driving the buckboard made the reply. "Got my whole cleanup! Thirty thousand dollars' worth of gold! One more like that and I'll be broke!"

Racing into the canyon, they churned to a halt at Hopalong's gesture and swung down. Hurrying through the rocks in the lead, Hopalong Cassidy stopped suddenly. His face slowly turned gray and hard.

Jesse Lock was dead. His gun was clutched in his hand, the muzzle tight against his temple!

"Suicide!" One of the men drew back. "He shot himself!"

"Looks like it," another man said, and Hopalong lifted his head slowly, having a feeling there had been almost satisfaction in the man's voice. But he could not make out which had been the speaker.

"Now what would make him do a thing like that?" It was the man who had first mentioned suicide. "It doesn't make sense!"

Hopalong moved swiftly away from the others, his hard blue eyes sweeping the ground, his lips twisted and bitter with the realization of failure. Yet what could he have done? The man had needed a doctor.

"Must have been in terrible pain," somebody commented. "Just had enough, I reckon."

The sheriff said nothing, and Hopalong stared at him curiously. When the old man did not speak, Hopalong said quietly, "He didn't kill himself. He was murdered."

"Murdered?" They all stared at him.

"He was murdered," Hopalong Cassidy repeated. "This man was alive and cheerful when I left him. He would not have shot himself."

"What's it look like to you, Hadley?" The speaker was a tall, bulky man with a broad red face. "If that isn't suicide, what is it? The gun's still in position."

Sheriff Hadley looked shrewdly at Hopalong and pulled his mustache thoughtfully. "He was alive when you left him? Was that gun within reach?"

"I put a gun in his hand. I didn't want to leave, but the man needed a doctor if he was goin' to live. I figure he might have made it."

Dr. Marsh had been examining the body. He looked up now. "That's true. Those wounds are in mighty healthy condition, everything considered. What's that poultice on them?"

"Prickly pear. Indians use it to check inflammation."

"Look!" The red-faced man indicated the

position of the gun. "If that isn't suicide, what would you call it?"

Hopalong felt anger mount within him. He looked up, his blue eyes utterly cold. "That man was alive when I left him," he repeated. "He knew he was hard hit, but he was standin' up to it. There wasn't"—he said the words viciously—"a single streak of yellow in that kid. He didn't kill himself.

"He must have passed out again," he continued. "Somebody sneaked down here, shot him with his own gun, then wrapped his fingers around it. Look where that gun muzzle is! Flush against his temple! Muzzle blast would have thrown that gun away from his head and maybe clear out of his hand!"

Dr. Marsh nodded. "This gentleman is correct, Hadley," he said quietly. "The recoil would have thrown it or jerked it away from the temple. Also, at that distance, the side of the face would have been badly burned. I can see only a few grains of powder in the skin."

The red-faced man was keeping his eyes on Cassidy. Slowly his gaze went over the black sombrero, shirt, and trousers tucked into high stitched boots, the tied-down, bone-handled guns, then climbed to his cold eyes and silver hair. "That puts you in a bad light," he suggested. "You were the last to see him alive."

"No." Hopalong's gaze was frosty. "The killer was the last to see him." He nodded back along the trail. "There's another one back there. Big fellow in a frock coat."

Hopalong was getting the men placed. The man who had driven the buckboard was Harrington, the mine super and part owner. It was on his shoulders the loss would fall. The big red-faced man was Pony Harper. He was a horse trader who owned the livery stable and corrals in Seven Pines and supplied beef to the mines and a railroad contracting outfit some thirty miles away. There was another man, hollow-cheeked, with yellow eyes and a tied-down gun; they called him Rawhide. He was searching the body in the road.

"Somebody cleaned him out!"

"What did you expect?" Hadley asked dryly. "This here was a robbery." Grimly, Hopalong said nothing. After what had happened to Jesse Lock, he wanted a chance to look over the contents of the man's wallet privately before he handed it over to anyone.

Another rider was coming up the trail from town. He was a well-built, pleasant-looking man of forty. "Howdy, Ronson!" Hadley nodded toward the dead man. "Anybody ever seen this hombre before?"

"I've seen him." Rawhide touched his tongue to a cigarette. "This man's Sim Thacker, the gunfighter."

"Thacker!" Ronson stared at the dead man. "Dead! Who did it?"

"That would answer a lot of other questions," Hadley said. "Looks like whoever did it gave him his chance, then drilled him."

"And put on the finishing touches with a bullet in the head," Hopalong said dryly. "That outfit seems to have an urge to leave no witnesses behind. They must figure folks might get to know them."

Nobody said anything for a while. Dr. Marsh examined Thacker, then got to his feet. "There's nothing more here for me," he said. "How about you, Harrington?"

The mine super shook his head. "Let's load them up and start back."

Hadley turned to Hopalong. "Stayin' around? Better be in Seven Pines for the inquest. It will be tomorrow."

"I'll be there. I'm ridin' in."

There was little talk as they headed toward Seven Pines, but what there was concerned the holdup gang and their previous work. The series of stage holdups had netted the gang just over a hundred thousand in gold, all of it in heavy bars. There was some talk of how it could be disposed of, for all possible places of sale had been alerted.

Harrington had been studying Cassidy. "You wear those guns like you understood 'em. I'll need a man to take Jesse's place as shotgun."

Hopalong chuckled. "From what I hear, that is not goin' to be a popular job. I hear your messengers die off mighty fast."

Harrington nodded soberly. "They do. I'll not deny that. I'd want a man who didn't scare easily. Jesse was gun-handy, all right. And too sure of himself. I always figured he had some ideas of his own about who the thieves were, but he wasn't talkative. Now he isn't able to do any talking to anybody."

"He said he had a brother in the Roberts range. Wanted him notified."

"Yeah. Ben Lock." Harrington shook his head. "He'll take it hard, and unless I miss my guess, the killers had better start worryin'. Ben's not the sort to take the death of his brother lyin' down."

The valley fell behind them and the buckboard led the way into a narrow canyon. Scattered mine dumps and shacks began to appear, and then the trail ended in a narrow street flanked by false-fronted buildings. Behind these buildings, which stretched for a quarter of a mile along the sides of the canyon, the mountains sloped steeply back, both sides covered with houses, claim shacks, and ramshackle huts of one kind or another.

The express office faced the livery stable across the street, and beside the express office a saloon stared bright-eyed at a general store. Up the street Hopalong noticed a saddle shop, bootmaker, blacksmith, barber and dentist, a lawyer's office, the jail, a hotel, a boarding-house, and an assortment of other stores and gambling joints. He counted the signs of nine saloons. At the far end of the street was the assayer's office.

Hopalong turned his horse toward the livery stable, and Harrington looked after him. "Don't forget! That job's open!"

Pony Harper and Rawhide had also turned off. Harper glanced at Hopalong curiously but said nothing. Rawhide swung from his saddle, and when Harper went into the livery stable office he said quietly, "I'd figure a long time before I took that messenger job. They seem to die awful easy."

"Maybe," Hopalong agreed, "somebody wants 'em to die."

"A feller could get into trouble stickin' around this town," Rawhide continued. "Montana's a good state. Ever been there?"

"Perhaps. I've been to a lot of places."

Rawhide kicked his boot toe into the earth and watched Hopalong stripping the saddle from Topper. "You sort of look familiar."

"That right?"

"Like somebody I seen in Montana. Or maybe it was Texas?"

"Never can tell."

Rawhide chewed that over, but he didn't like it. Locally he was known as a hard character, and he fancied the reputation. He did not like his questions being avoided. Besides, he had an uneasy feeling that this was a man whom he should know. Whom it was important to know. He rolled a smoke and shot an uneasy glance at Hopalong, who was placidly giving his horse a rubdown with a handful of hay.

"Lock have much to say?" he ventured.

"Said he had a brother," Hopalong admitted. "I'm goin' to look him up."

"Mister, you better slope it. This here ain't a friendly town."

"Well"—Hopalong Cassidy's eyes twinkled a little—"I'm not huntin' trouble with anybody." He turned and started for the door. "So long."

"Hold up there!" Rawhide was angry now. "I asked you a question and I want an answer!"

Cassidy stopped and turned slowly, facing the man in the half-light of the livery stable.

"What did Lock have to say?" Rawhide repeated. "I could beat it out of you!"

Instantly he knew he had said the wrong thing. Hopalong Cassidy took a step toward him. "All right," he agreed, "you beat it out of me. But start now. I'm in no mood for waitin'."

Rawhide swallowed, touched his dry lips with his tongue, and his face became somber. Suddenly he realized this man would not bluff and he would not scare. Fairly called, Rawhide found he did not want trouble. Not now, not here.

"Oh, shucks!" he said. "I was just funnin'! It don't make any difference, only I figured maybe he talked and said something interestin'. I'm not huntin' for trouble. You're plumb on the prod."

Hopalong watched him without speaking, waiting. Rawhide shifted his feet nervously, wanting to stride up to this man and strike him, to threaten him with a gun, anything. He wanted to, but a deep-seated judgment warned him it would not be advisable to try.

Hopalong gave him one more look and

turned on his heel. Coolly, without a backward glance, he walked out into the sunlit street.

Rawhide stared after him, his eyes ugly. "You'll see," he whispered. "I give you twenty-four hours in this town!"

CHAPTER 2

RAMROD OF THE ROCKING R

As Hopalong vanished through the wide-mouthed door Pony Harper stepped from the deep shadows of a stall. As he strode up to Rawhide his face was dark with irritation. "You fool!" he said. "Why brace him about what Lock said? What difference does it make what he said, or whether he said anything at all? If he did say anything, this hombre will tell it, and if he didn't, there's no use makin' the man suspicious."

"Aw, shucks!" Rawhide replied sullenly. "Who's he to get suspicious?"

"Who he is," Harper said unpleasantly, "I don't know, but don't you push trouble with that hombre unless you want to throw lead. That's one gent who's not bluffin'!"

Harper turned on his heel and left the

fuming gunman behind him. Despite his words, he was worried. That Jesse Lock had talked before he died was obvious. He had taken time to tell this stranger about his brother, and he might have said more. Still, what could he have seen on such a night? What would he have to tell? It was barely possible he had recognized someone, but that chance was small. The best course was to sit tight and see what would develop . . . give this stranger time to drift out of the country.

Worst of all, Thacker was dead, and the manner of his death sent a cold chill up Harper's spine. Had they guessed his mission? Or had Thacker himself spoken?

Hopalong Cassidy headed for the nearest saloon, then changed his course. A sign down the street advertised: KATIE REGAN FOR STEAK, EGGS, AND PIE. He went up the boardwalk and pushed open the door. Except for a cowhand in run-down boots and a ragged hat who slept with his head pillowed on his arms, the place seemed to be empty.

The bell that tinkled to warn of his coming did not disturb the cowhand but brought a girl with a very pretty face from the kitchen. Her black hair was gathered atop a beautifully shaped head, and her blue eyes were flecked with darker color. She inspected him curiously, and he grinned response. "Howdy! I'll take the steak, eggs, and pie."

She came into the room holding a large ladle and pushing up a strand of hair. "Don't give me that!" she said severely. " 'Tis steak and pie, or eggs and pie, and either will cost you two bits!"

"Bring me both of 'em," Hopalong said seriously. "The biggest, thickest, juiciest steak you've got, and make that four eggs instead of two! If you've got some beans, throw in a mess of them."

"The beans go with either order, but that order will cost you six bits. Have you got that much?"

"If I haven't," he said, grinning, "I'll wash dishes!"

"Oh, no, you don't!" she flashed. "Every cowhand this side of Dakota has tried that! And then when they get into the kitchen it isn't washing dishes they think of! You'll pay—and cash!"

Hopalong's dollar rang on the tabletop. "All right, Katie! Feed me!"

Swiftly she scooped up the dollar and dropped it in her apron pocket. "Sit down and

I'll be right back." She turned. "How do you want that steak?"

"Just dehorn it and run it in, Katie. I'll take it from there."

Frying steak spluttered, and then she reappeared with a steaming cup of coffee. She was a tall girl with a superb figure, and Hopalong had no trouble imagining that many drifting cowhands had tried that dishwashing trick. "You're new here?" she ventured. "Are you the one who found Jesse Lock?"

He nodded. "News gets around. Did you know him?"

"I knew him. There's not a hand this side of Texas that's his equal. And good with a gun, too, although in that they say he can't hold a candle to his brother Ben."

Hopalong waited, wanting her to go on talking. There were times when listening paid off. He intended to look around a bit before leaving. The murder of Jesse Lock had become a personal matter now. Had Lock died from the original shots, Cassidy would not have considered it any of his affair, but to have the man so foully murdered while Hopalong was doing his best to save him was quite something else. He would like to have a look at the man who would do such a thing.

"What will Harrington do for a shotgun rider now?" he queried.

Katie Regan looked down at him. "They do say he offered the job to you."

"Uh-huh. I'm not job huntin', and if I take a job, it will be ridin'."

Katie returned to the kitchen and came back with the steak and eggs. While he ate, Katie talked. *"Nobody* hiring much now. Ronson needs riders. He can never keep any around with those two sisters of his."

"Bob Ronson?" Hopalong looked up. "He was out there today with Hadley and Harper."

"That was the one. He owns the Rocking R, and it's a good ranch, although it's said that he's hard-pressed for money."

"You mentioned girls?"

Katie flashed Hopalong a glance. "I thought that would get you. Every cowhand in the country tries to get a job there, and everyone tries to dab a rope on one or the other of the girls, although Lenny seems to be the preferred one. Irene has a way about her that scares them a little. Anyway, she seems spoken for."

"Pretty, are they?"

"No, not just pretty. They are beautiful."

Hopalong nodded seriously. He was not thinking of the Ronson sisters. He was trying to get a line on this town and the country around it. He wanted to know just what went on. Sheriff Hadley was a good man, he would gamble on that. How much imagination he would have was another guess.

While he ate, Hopalong kept Katie Regan talking, and the community began to take shape in Hopalong's mind. His keen blue eyes were thoughtful as he listened.

The community was a combination of cattle and mining. The biggest cow outfit was Bob Ronson's Rocking R; the only mine of any consequence was Harrington's Gold Stake. Ronson had inherited the Rocking R from his father, who had been an old gray wolf from the high timber, a man who had teeth and used them on the least provocation. He had been honest in his dealings, but utterly ruthless. The Rocking R had made few friends and many enemies. When the old man died, rustlers hit the Rocking R high, low, and in the middle.

Within a year two of the Rocking R hands had been dry-gulched and more than a thousand head of cattle run off.

Small outfits that had heretofore scarcely made their way began to wax fat, their herds growing, their shipments getting larger. Their owners began to spend more money as the Rocking R spent less. New faces were seen around the country, too, and where the Rock-ing R hands under the firm leadership of Old Man Ronson had kept the town cleaned up, now there were many loafers and hangers-on, most of whom had money or seemed to know how to get it.

The Gold Stake was booming and many restless eyes began to look thoughtfully toward the monthly gold shipments that went out by stage. Meanwhile, the Ronson cattle herds, while still vast, had thinned down. Rustlers took to fighting over them, and one night four known rustlers were killed on the Rocking R range by other rustlers.

Small mines began to pay off, and two of them were looted after cleanups. In one case the owner was killed. In another, masked men had beaten two of the workers at the mine and taken gold from them. A prospector was mur-dered for his outfit. A freight wagon was looted on the outskirts of town and the teamster mur-dered. From a quiet community under the rough hand of Ronson, the area had become wild, lawless, and almost beyond handling. Sheriff Hadley had replaced the previous sher-iff, who had been dry-gulched in the town it-self.

"There's always a ringleader," Hopalong suggested. "Who is it runs Seven Pines?"

"Nobody, actually. The ranchers used to follow Ronson, but lately they have been listening more and more to Pony Harper."

"The horse trader?"

"That's the one, but he owns a small ranch, too, and he is a cattle buyer as well as owner of the livery stable. There's also Sheriff Hadley, of course, and Dr. Marsh."

There were footsteps on the boardwalk and Katie glanced out the window. "This here's Clarry Jacks coming in now," she said, moving away from Hopalong. "He's someone that the *newer* element around here have been following more and more."

Before he could ask what she meant, the door opened and two men walked into the room. The first was a black-browed, bowlegged man with a thick body and deep-set black eyes. Yet it was the man behind him who drew Hopalong's attention.

Clarry Jacks was handsome. Gray eyes and chestnut hair, a lithe, erect figure, and an easy, carefree walk made him the natural focus of attention. He wore two silver-plated, pearl-handled guns tied down in elaborate hand-carved holsters.

"Howdy, Katie!" Jacks grinned widely. "Set 'em up for us, will you? Two cups of coffee and a half dozen of those sinkers of yours!"

"You set down, Clarry," Katie said severely, "and you'll get waited on same as anybody else. The same for your friend"—she shot a glance at Hoppy—"Dud Leeman."

Hopalong glanced at Jacks, who had turned toward him. "Stranger?" Jacks asked.

"Have you seen me around before?" Hopalong asked coolly.

"No. That's why I asked."

"If you haven't seen me around before, I must be a stranger." Hopalong smiled. Turning back toward Katie, he asked quietly, "How's for another cup of java? You sure make good coffee."

Jacks was irritated at this flouting of his importance and he showed it. He started to say something more, then hesitated. Leeman was staring at Cassidy and frowning, seemingly puzzled, but he offered no comment. Ignoring the stranger, Jacks turned back to his coffee and doughnuts. He had not failed to notice Hopalong's bone-handled, tied-down guns. Whoever the fellow was, he was no pilgrim.

Hopalong finished his coffee and strolled outside. He had recognized Jacks at once, seeing beyond the easy laughter to the underlying hardness of the man. On the surface Jacks might seem gay and friendly to many, but he was the sort of man who could be utterly ruthless. Match that to gun skill, and it could mean a lot of trouble.

The High-Grade Saloon showed down the street a few doors, and Hopalong drifted that way.

In the door of Katie Regan's, Dud Leeman stared after him, watching the short, choppy horseman's walk, the sloping but powerful shoulders, and the tied-down guns. He slammed the door and strode back to the counter. Clarry Jacks stared at him curiously. "What's eatin' you?" He grinned. "That hombre scare you?"

"Scare, nothin'!" Leeman dropped to a stool and spooned sugar into his coffee. "Only he seems durned familiar. I've seen him somewhere but can't remember where."

Clarry Jacks shrugged. "Just a driftin' hand. He'll move on."

"He'll stick around." Katie had come in from the kitchen. "At least for a while. The murder of that boy got under his skin."

"Does he think he can do better than the sheriff?" Jacks wanted to know.

"I don't know whether he can do better than Hadley or not," she replied easily, "but if I was the killer I'd be feeling mighty uneasy."

. . .

Circulating around through the various saloons and hangouts, Hopalong kept his eyes and ears open. Long ago he had learned to know the signs of a tough town, and he could see this one was seething. He heard of several killings, of a slugging and robbery the previous night, of another prospector found dead on his claim. The lid was off and the wolves were flocking to the fat herd.

As long as he lived, Old Cattle Bob Ronson had kept the town under his thumb. It had been he and his hands who enforced the law, and now he was gone. Young Bob was admitted to be an excellent cowman but no fighter. The town was wide open and the trouble was only starting.

Over a bottle, Hopalong talked to an old cowhand who nodded grimly toward Joe Turner, the fat, bald-pated man behind the bar whose gold watch chain crossed an imposing stomach. "He's ridin' high with Old Cattle Bob dead!" he sneered. "No sound out of him when the old man was around, but now he's playin' it mighty big!"

Cassidy strolled on to the bar, recording in his memory the cowhand's comment. Bill Harrington was standing there, and he turned, smiling, when he saw Cassidy. "Glad to see you, amigo," he said quietly. "Changed your mind about ridin' shotgun for me?"

Hopalong shook his bead. "Not yet. I'll be stayin' around awhile, but I'd prefer a ridin' job. I may hit Ronson about it. Who is his foreman?"

"Handles the job himself. He knows cows and he knows range. He don't like trouble, though, and doesn't have the backbone for this. You can see why." Harrington gestured toward the room. "At least sixty men in here right now. I'd bet at least twenty of them have killed their man, some of them several. Probably more than that are cow thieves. Another ten would be crooked gamblers. It's no job for a tenderfoot.

"Over there"—he indicated Joe Turner— "is the man who would like to run the town. He isn't big enough."

"Who is?"

Harrington glanced at Cassidy and smiled. "That, my friend, is a good question. Some of them think I am, but I don't want the job, believe me. I'd sooner ride shotgun on my own shipments."

He shook his head. "No, there's no man

big enough now. Doc Marsh has the brains and courage, but he doesn't have either the leadership or the desire. His practice suits him. Hadley just can't do it."

"What about Pony Harper?" Cassidy asked casually.

Harrington hesitated. "There," he said at last, "you may have something, but Harper's not an easy man to understand."

Cassidy changed the subject. "What about that gold of yours? How will the thieves get rid of it? Gold isn't the easiest thing to handle. Not in quantity."

"You're right, and I've good reason to believe that not a single ounce of stolen gold has appeared on the market anywhere. My idea is, their plans were made before the gold was ever stolen, but it will take some managing."

Harrington shrugged, then waved a hand at the room. "And whom to suspect? Any of them! This room is filled with thieves! Believe me, Ben Lock will have his work cut out for him!"

He glanced around as somebody shouted a welcome. "Here's Young Bob Ronson now, if you want that job. Hit him up for it."

Ronson was a tall, well-made young man with a pleasant, friendly face. He walked to the bar, strolling over near Harrington. "How are you, Bill?" He shot a quick, measuring glance at Cassidy. "You're the man who found Lock."

"That's right," Cassidy said, "and I was fixin' to ask if you needed a hand."

Ronson laughed. "I need lots of them, friend. Lots of them! But I'd better warn you that being a hand for the Rocking R isn't a popular occupation right now. Somebody seems to have decided to eliminate them."

"I've been shot at before," Hopalong said.

"All right. Come out in the morning." He started to turn away and then hesitated. "By the way, what's your handle?"

"Cassidy. My friends call me Hopalong."

Harrington straightened up and stared. Ronson had stopped in mid-stride, and somebody, somewhere nearby, swore. Hopalong had not spoken loudly, yet there had been a sudden lull, and at least a dozen men had heard him. That the name meant nothing to some of them was obvious, but that it meant a great deal to Harrington, Ronson, and Dud Leeman was also obvious.

"Hopalong Cassidy . . ." Ronson stared. "Man, I'll say you've got a job! Come out in the morning, by all means!"

Dud Leeman had turned swiftly. He strode from the room. Hopalong glanced after him curiously. The dark-skinned gunman had

seemed unusually upset. Harrington had noticed it, too, but said nothing. Pony Harper
stood nearby, but his back was toward them,
and whether he had heard, neither man knew.

"In the morning then." Hopalong nodded
to the men, then turned and moved through
the crowd toward the door.

The Rocking R lay in a notch of the
Antelopes, a rambling, Spanish-style house
sprawling comfortably among the cottonwoods
with a huge old log barn, a series of pole corrals, and a bunkhouse that trailed a lazy thread
of smoke toward the sky. A great tank, almost a
half acre in extent, was placid with crystal-clear
water. Green moss showed at the edges, and a
thin trickle dribbled into the tank from a pipe.
After the trail Topper was ready for the water,
and he sank his muzzle into it as Hopalong
swung down. Sunlight reflected from the green
leaves of the cottonwoods, and Hopalong
heard a door slam from the house and looked
across the saddle at the girl walking toward
him.

She walked as gracefully and easily as a
fawn. Her hair was brown but red-tinged in the
sunlight, and her face and throat were lightly,

beautifully tanned. She was young, probably seventeen, but rounded and perfect. She was, as Katie Regan had said, beautiful.

She smiled, her quick green eyes studying him. "Are you Cassidy? Bob said to tell you to locate a bunk, stow your gear, and then just look the place over. He's off across the range and won't be back until night. He said you'd want to get acquainted with the ranch."

"Thanks." Hopalong smiled. "I reckon he's right, at that. A man always feels better around a place once he knows the lay of the land. You run many cows?"

Her smile disappeared. "We did—and when it comes to that, we still do. I expect there's a good many thousand head on the place, but some of the boys around are a little on the rustle since Dad died."

"So I hear. Don't the hands stop it?"

"They tried, but the ones who tried didn't last long. They were killed mighty fast." She was bitter. "What this ranch needs is a fighting foreman! Somebody who would really run it!"

"Well, maybe. And again maybe not. That sort of thing can lead to a lot of trouble unless your fightin' foreman has judgment too."

"If Irene didn't side with Bob all the time, we'd have one!" The girl's eyes flashed. "I've tried to get Bob to hire Clarry Jacks! He'd be the man! They wouldn't run over us then!"

"Jacks?" Hopalong was surprised. He looked the girl over more carefully. "Maybe he would be the man, but he doesn't size it up to me, ma'am. Of course I'm only a stranger here. What does this Jacks do?"

"Do?" She looked at Hopalong, momentarily puzzled and, he thought, a little confused. "What do you mean?"

"I mean what does he do for a livin'? Is he a puncher?"

"Why, he has been. Right now he isn't doing anything."

Hopalong nodded thoughtfully. "I see." He slid the saddle from Topper. "That's a right nice job, but it don't pay much. A man can only do it so long and then he's broke. Of course I expect Jacks doesn't need much money. If you have friends around, a man can live off them."

Her eyes flashed. "Why! Why, that's not fair! How can you say a thing like that?"

Hopalong looked innocent. He was momentarily sorry he had spoken so and was not quite sure why he had. For all he knew, Clarry Jacks might be a pillar of society. Only if he were, then all Hopalong's instincts were at fault.

"Perhaps I was wrong, ma'am," he said apologetically. "Only a man has to make a livin' somehow. He rides for somebody, owns a ranch, prospects, works in a mine, tends bar, or something. Maybe Jacks has an income or something. I don't know."

Lenny Ronson eyed him without pleasure. Her continued championing of Jacks had irritated her brother and worried her sister. Nevertheless, the dashing gunman appealed to her. He was so fearless, yet so gay. He was far from the cool, quiet man her brother was, and Lenny was full of fire herself and furious that the ranch could be stolen blind while her brother did nothing.

The only solution for the Rocking R was to make Clarry Jacks foreman. Then the stealing would be ended in a hurry. Yet, although they possessed equal shares, her brother had been given complete control over the operation of the ranch. It had been so provided in Cattle Bob's will. To make matters worse, from Lenny's point of view, Irene almost always sided with Bob when they discussed matters of ranch policy.

"That's a beautiful horse," Lenny said, changing the subject.

Cassidy nodded with real pleasure. "He

sure is! Best cutting horse I ever rode, an' I've ridden some. Got more brains than most humans."

"Are you staying long? I mean, did Bob hire you just for the roundup?"

"Don't rightly know," Hopalong mused. "Nothin' was mentioned about what I was to do or the time I'd be here. I heard he needed hands, so hit him for the job."

"Did you hear that we had lost some hands?" Lenny demanded. "Did Bob tell you that?"

"Yeah, he mentioned it, and some other folks did." Hopalong let his eyes run over the sunlit hills and drew a deep breath of the fresh, dancing spring air. "I reckon every range has its troubles."

He carried the saddle under a shed and threw it across a pole kept for the purpose, hanging up the bridle and bit. "How many hands have you got now?"

"Only five. We used to have anywhere from twelve to twenty on this place." Lenny's voice was bitter. "It's the biggest ranch around here."

"They been workin' here long?"

"Only two of them. Frenchy Ruyters and Tex Milligan. Frenchy has been with us since I was a child. Tex hired on about four years ago."

"What about the others?"

"You'd better decide for yourself. You'll have to work with them. They are good hands, I think. Kid Newton has been with us about two weeks. The others hired on about a month ago. They are saddle partners, Joe Hartley and Dan Dusark."

She was silent for several minutes while Hopalong studied the ranch with careful, appraising eyes. The buildings and the grounds were well kept; the stock he had seen was in good shape. Whatever Bob Ronson might not be as a fighter, he was no rawhider as a rancher. He believed in running a good place, and he did. This, in good times, could be a fine place to work.

"We'll have trouble," Lenny said soberly, "at the roundup. We'd be less than honest if we didn't tell you. There's an outfit east of here who are getting too big for their hats. Three brothers named Gore from over on Blue Mountain."

"What's the trouble?"

"They want range. Bob thinks they are a little on the rustle too. So does Tex. Anyway, they've been pushing our stock off land the Rocking R has used for twenty years. Tex braced them about it and they invited him to start something. All three of them were present, and they laughed at him, trying to egg him into going for a gun so they could kill him.

"John is the worst, I think. But there's little to choose. Windy and Con are almost as bad. They've boasted they'll run the Rocking R off the range."

There was a rattle of horses' hoofs, and glancing up, Hopalong saw Bob Ronson come riding into the place with three hands beside him. The dark, lean-faced man with the shrewd eyes would be Frenchy Ruyters; the narrow-hipped youngster could be nobody but Tex Milligan, for his state was written all over him. Bob Ronson introduced them by saying their names. The last was a big-bodied man with a round, sullen face. His name was Dan Dusark.

"Startin' today," Ronson said abruptly, "Cassidy's segundo on this ranch. Take his orders like you would my own. Cassidy, we'll talk inside." Swinging down, Ronson led off at a rapid walk.

Inside, Bob Ronson stopped by his desk and shoved his hands down into his pockets. His eyes twinkled and he grinned suddenly. "Hopalong," he said, "I've heard stories about you for a long time. Gibson of the Three T L talks about you all the time. Now you're here, and believe me, you're a godsend. Making you segundo of this spread is throwing a load on your shoulders, but if what he says is true, you're just the man for the job.

"You'll be stepping into trouble. We're the big outfit, we're short of cash, and we're being robbed blind. The small ranches are range-hungry and over half of them rustling.

"You're a fighter. I know men. I knew when I saw you out there after the holdup that Gibson was right. You'll give the orders when it means fighting. To me as well as the others. I can handle cattle, but I've no confidence in my ability to handle a war. That's your job."

Cassidy nodded. His admiration for this lean, sincere cattleman was growing.

"You expect trouble from the Gores too?"

"You heard of them? Yes, I do. And from other sources there will be trouble. We're the melon they all want to cut in to."

"All right," Cassidy agreed, hitching his gun belts, "you've hired a hand. I'll run it through without gun smoke if I can. And if I can't?"

"Use your own discretion," Ronson said simply. "They are asking for trouble. If they want it, give it to them. Only"—his eyes hardened—"if they start it, we win it. Understand?"

CHAPTER 3

HOPALONG
SERVES NOTICE

The truth of the matter was that Hopalong Cassidy enjoyed ranch life. It was not only association that made it so, but a deep-seated and genuine appreciation for what he was doing. He liked cattle and thoroughly understood them. He liked horses, and good or bad, he enjoyed working with them. Already in his short life he had seen changes come to the range and he was well aware that the life he lived was not to last forever.

Where once there had been unlimited miles of unfenced and unsettled range, now fences were coming up and nesters creeping in. In some places the nester would remain. In others he would leave, for much of the western grass country was never made for farming. Once it was plowed, the wind ripped into it and turned the prairie into a vast dustbin where billowing clouds obscured the sun. But whether he stayed or departed, the nester and the small rancher were bringing changes into the free range country of the West.

Many of them were honest, home-loving people who wanted nothing more than to make a living. For such as these Hopalong had respect. There were others, however, who came only to fatten themselves and their herds on the vaster herds of the big cattlemen, to reap what others had sown, to spend what others had earned.

These last were of two principal types: the out-and-out rustler, who drove off herds, took his chances with the cattlemen and would shoot it out if cornered, and the other type, who covered his stealing under a veil of appearances, and allied himself to the honest men of the community. To such as these a ranch like the Rocking R was a veritable honey pot.

Cattle Bob's death was reported far and wide by word of mouth, and into the country had flocked those who wished to fatten from his herds. The first raids had been tentative, testing raids to see if the young cub carried the punishing claws of the old bear. They soon found he did not, and then the looting began. By the time Hopalong Cassidy arrived it was in full swing, and instead of driving cattle off by the dozen, the steals were rising in scope until nights came when several hundred head were driven off at once, and often by several different gangs.

To some of them the name of Hopalong Cassidy was known. No newspaper had published reports of his activities, for no newspaper was necessary. Drifting hands, stage drivers, cattle buyers, and all the vast itinerant army of the western country had carried the news. They knew the manner of man he was and the speed with which he used his guns. Most of these stories centered in the range country of the great plains east of the Rockies. However, as such stories always do, these had drifted westward through the mountain passes from Wyoming and down from Montana until the name was known to a few at least.

Here and there among the ranks of the outlaws were those who had actually encountered him before. It was noteworthy, and should have been thought-provoking, that these were the first to drift. One tough hand who worked for the Gores on their 3 G spread heard the name at sundown.

He looked up quickly from his plate.

"Hopalong's here?" He was incredulous, worried.

"Yeah, that's his name." John Gore was not impressed. He had never heard of Cassidy nor of the old Bar 20 outfit.

The tough hand got to his feet. "Boss," he said quietly, "I reckon I want my time. I'm driftin'."

"Quittin'?" Gore was amazed, and the others looked up too. "What's the matter, Slim?"

"Matter?" Slim stared at him. "Look, John. I'm as tough as the next, but I ain't no fool. I know Hopalong Cassidy. I ain't buckin' him for any price. He's a curly gray wolf from the high timber, and anyway, I feel like driftin' south where there's more sun."

"Shucks, it's only spring now. Wait another month or so and you'll get all the sun you want."

"Maybe. But right now I feel mighty cold."

"If you ask me," Con Gore said harshly, "it's your feet gettin' cold."

Slim turned on him. "That's right, Con. They are. I'd rather be alive with forty bucks in my kick than dead with four hundred. You stay here, and the day will come when you'll wish to heaven you'd drifted with me!"

．　　　．　　　．

For three days Hopalong scouted the range. Once he rode west toward the Black Sand Desert, which barred the cattle from further travel that way. But mostly his rides took him toward Haystack Valley and the distant Blue Mountains. As he rode he studied the range and the country. Spring rains had been good, and the cattle were already increasing in weight. The range was well cared for, the ponds cleaned out and shored up, the water holes and springs deepened, the washes dammed to stop the wasting of soil as well as to impound water. Young Bob Ronson was a thoughtful and intelligent man, a rancher who, given peace, would prosper.

The home ranch lay on the western slope of the Antelopes, but a small pass gave easy outlet to the vast range to their east where many of the cattle ran. It was upon this range where the battle with the Gores had opened. Not only were cattle missing, but the Gore brothers were pushing their own cows onto range that had always been used by the Rocking R.

Southward, Rocking R cattle ranged as far as Poker Gap and Cow Creek Canyon, and westward to the Black Sand Desert. Southeastward, as Frenchy Ruyters had told Hopalong, lay the outlaw village of Corn Patch. Sometimes it was deserted, sometimes crowded. "And now?" Hopalong asked.

"Crowded," Frenchy replied grimly, "like coyotes flockin' to a fresh kill. Those Gores, they worry me more than the regular outlaws. The three of them are tough as mule hide and poison-mean. They take to trouble like a bear to a berry patch, and they are slippier than a mustang on a blue clay sidehill!"

"We'll see 'em," Hopalong said easily. "We'll talk to 'em."

"Well, you won't have to wait," Frenchy replied dryly. "Here they come."

Tex Milligan drifted his pony down off the hillside. "Here comes Windy Gore and some of his hands."

The riders were four in number, and they came swiftly. Hopalong was riding Topper and he swung the white gelding to face them and walked him forward a full length toward the oncoming riders.

"Howdy," he said quietly. "I take it you're Windy Gore?"

The tallest of the men, a lean, sour-faced man with a lantern jaw stared at him. "You take it right. And you're on 3 G range."

Hopalong smiled. "According to my information, this here's the Rocking R. All of it, clear to the Blues. Seems to me this outfit was here a long time before the 3 G outfit. How do you explain that?"

"I don't!" Windy Gore laughed loudly. "Old Cattle Bob rode right over his neighbors while he was alive, but he ain't alive anymore. Now get off and stay off!"

Hopalong sat his saddle. Coolly he let his gaze stray over the Gore riders, fixing first one and then another with his cold blue eyes.

"Windy," he said quietly, "this is Rocking R range. It continues to be Rocking R range. There's plenty of land east of the Blues if you want to run some stock. I'd advise you to get hold of it before somebody else does. If you and your brothers want to live peacefully, we can get along. If you want war, there's no need to wait; you can start it right now."

"Huh?" Windy Gore was startled. Hopalong had spoken so quietly that it was a few seconds before the import of his statement penetrated Windy's consciousness. When it did, rage flooded him, and yet along with the rage was a cold thread of reason. The odds were not good enough. Cassidy was supposed to be dangerous, and certainly there was no weakness to be expected from Frenchy or Tex. They might not be gun-slick, but they would stand hitched. Windy Gore was not so foolish as to buck a deck stacked the way this one was. Especially as he knew that he himself would be the first target of all three men. It was an uncomfortable thought.

"You heard me." Hopalong pushed his horse forward until it stood shoulder to shoulder with Gore's. "I said it could be peace or war, any way you want it, and no need to wait. You boys have been makin' war talk. Now make up your minds. If you want it, you can have it."

Behind and to the left of Windy a sullen-faced man sat his horse. Partly bald, he had a brutal jaw and small eyes above heavy cheekbones. "Let me have him, Windy," this man begged. "Just let me have—"

The sentence was never completed, for Hopalong swung a wicked backhand blow against the man's chin that rocked him in the saddle. His right foot slipped from the stirrup, and swooping, Hopalong grabbed it and jerked high. Caught unexpectedly by the sudden action, the bald-headed man slipped from the saddle and hit the dust with a crash. Instantly Hopalong was off his horse, and before the man could even gain his feet, Hoppy grabbed his shirt front with his left hand and jerked him up into a wicked right. Then he dropped the fellow and stepped back.

Stunned, the bald-headed man shook his head; then with awakening realization he came off the ground with a grunt. He came up fast, and Hopalong swung a sweeping left that split his cheek to the bone and then a right that thudded on his chin, and the man went down on his face in the dust.

Stepping back, Hopalong saw that Milligan's rifle was over his saddle, covering the others. "There it is, Gore," Cassidy said, breathing easily. "Your man asked for it and he got it."

"You'll not get away with this!" Windy was furious, but wary. The odds had changed still more now, for the man on the ground was not stirring. Even if he were on his feet he would be in no shape to hold up his end in a gun battle.

"Tell your brothers there's plenty of range here for all of us. Just keep your cattle across the Blues and keep your hands off Rocking R cows. We don't want trouble, but we're ready for it."

The beaten man was sitting up, shaking his head to clear it of fog. He looked up, his eyes ugly with hatred. "Next time," he snarled, "it will be guns!"

"Why wait?" Hopalong faced him abruptly. "You've got a gun. If you want to die, reach for it."

For a long moment the man stared, his fingers twitching with eagerness. Hopalong saw the desire to kill in his eyes, then saw it die slowly. "Not now," the man said. "Later."

"All right, then," Cassidy said coolly. He raised his eyes to Windy's. "Any time I find any rider from the 3 G on this range, either armed or with a running iron or rope, he loses his horse and walks home!"

"What?" Windy bellowed. "Why, you—"

He gulped his words, seeing the ice in Cassidy's eyes. "Go ahead!" Hopalong invited. "Start somethin'. You can ride back over a saddle as easy as astride one!"

When the four had ridden away, Tex Milligan chuckled. "Man! Did you see Windy's face? He was fit to be tied! That's the first time anybody faced up to a Gore, and believe me, it didn't set well!"

Ruyters grinned, but his eyes were worried. "Served 'em right," he agreed, "but they'll come a-gunnin' now. They've got more hands than we have."

They started their horses on and Hopalong let his eyes search the range. This was dry country. Even now, in the spring of the year when it was at its best, it offered little. Sagebrush mingled with bunch wheat grass and here and there solid patches of winter fat. Its whitish, almost light-gray color could be discerned at considerable distance, and it was one of the most valuable grazing plants of this sort of range. Yet some hillsides were already badly washed, and the country, despite the winter fat, would support but few cattle in relation to the vast area.

The wheat grass and sagebrush offered good spring range, and cattle here might be fattened well before the heat of the summer and the scarcity of water hit them.

Frenchy had been noticing Hopalong's study of the range. "She don't look much," he agreed, as if reading Cassidy's thoughts, "but that winter fat is good range, and there's lots of it. North of the home ranch there's a couple of valleys chock-full of it, and it stands grazing mighty well."

Frenchy added, "Ronson has an idea that's a good one, I reckon. He figures that in late spring, when it begins to get hot and dry, he'll drive his cattle north across the desert and into the High Rock Canyon country. Lots of good grass and water up there. He's worked out a deal with a rancher up there by the name of Gibson."

"I know him," Hopalong said. "Drove over the trail the same time that he did. Knew his son-in-law."

They rode in silence for a while, and then Hopalong asked suddenly, "Any loose riders around that we could hire? Good hands who will fight?"

Tex Milligan shrugged. "Maybe a couple. Shorty Montana's around town. He's a fightin' son of a gun when he gets unwound. Tough little squirt. He wouldn't work for Young Bob, though. Turned him down twice. Had some sort of a run-in with the old man."

"Serious?"

"Naw, just a couple of fire-eaters. Shorty would walk into any kind of trouble with guns a-smokin' if he figured he wanted to or if there was anybody in there he wanted. Him and Jesse Lock were pretty thick, but Shorty hits the bottle hard when he's off the job."

"How about when he's workin'?"

"Never touches it. Kind of quarrelsome ranny. He likes trouble and hunts it, so he doesn't have so much as you'd figure. Never saw such an hombre for fightin'."

"Win?"

"Fifty-fifty. He don't seem to care much. He just likes it. One hombre licked him three times over at Unionville. Every Saturday night

Shorty would go back and tackle him again. Hombre finally left the country to get away from him."

Gently, Hopalong chuckled. It might pay to ride in and have a talk with Shorty Montana.

"Where does he hang out?"

"Katie Regan's, mostly. The Nevada Saloon other times."

A thin trail of smoke invited their attention, and they drifted that way.

Kid Newton looked up from his fire. His rifle lay close by and he was wearing a gun. He was a slim, awkward boy, but his grin was wide. "Howdy!" he said. "Light and sit! Got coffee on, and grub comin' up." He glanced at Hopalong. "I saw what happened down yonder. I was close by."

Cassidy looked him over with new attention. "Close by? Where were you?"

"Behind a rock about three hundred yards off. Had me a dead bead on Windy Gore."

Frenchy Ruyters indicated the boy with his head. "The kid's good with a rifle, Hoppy. I've seen him drop an antelope at three hundred yards with the antelope runnin' full tilt. Shoots 'em right in the head."

"Aw, that ain't anythin'!" Newton was embarrassed. "I've been shootin' all my life."

Milligan poured coffee into a tin cup and

handed it to Hopalong. "Go easy on that," he said. "We panned some of it out once and found after the water was poured off that she assayed forty percent coffee, forty percent alkali, ten percent assorted minerals, and ten percent gold.

"Fellers," he said seriously, "always panned their coffee before they drunk it. Many a cowhand in this here country's made him a stake thataway."

Frenchy snorted. "You pay too much attention to Tex," he said, "and his stories'll make your head hurt."

Milligan snorted. "Me? Tell stories? Why, Hoppy," he exclaimed, "this hombre won't even believe what I tell him about that hundred-mile bob-wire fence on the XIT. I know it's there! I helped stretch her myself!

"They unrolled three strands of wire for a hundred miles. Unbroken stretch of it. Then we hitched an ox team to each end of it, and stretched her tight. We worked by smoke signals, and we stretched that wire so tight that it wasn't until four years after that we had to put the posts up!

"Fact is," he continued, "I don't think we needed 'em then, but the boss figured it would look better to have more than the two anchor posts at each end."

"Drink your coffee," Ruyters said disgustedly, "and shut up!"

Hopalong grinned and tried his own coffee. He wrinkled his nose at the flavor. Whether there was gold in it he did not know, but it tasted strongly of alkali. He grinned. If he had all the sand and dust that he had drunk in camp coffee stretched out in one layer, he would have had enough for a ranch of his own.

Ruyters turned to Cassidy. "Hoppy," he said, "I've worked with this cap-rock turkey for a couple of years now. Can't you let me work with the kid or somebody else? Those stories of his would drive a man to drink."

"Say," Newton said suddenly, glancing up from the fire, "I hear that feller Jacks has staked him a claim over on Ghost Mountain east of Corn Patch!"

"Jacks?" Ruyters puckered his brow. "Didn't know he was a miner."

"Ghost Mountain?" Hopalong asked, looking over at Kid Newton. "Why the ghost part?"

"Supposed to be haunted. Used to be a minin' town over there by the name of Star City. She died out about 1868, but there were a couple of fellers who fell into a shaft up there on the mountain and starved to death before they were found. Folks say their ghosts have been seen. Me, I figure it's just a story some of that Corn Patch outfit put out."

"I hear that's a tough place," Cassidy said.

Frenchy Ruyters nodded agreement. "It is at any time. Poker Harris runs a sort of store, saloon, and gamblin' joint there. Hangout for outlaws. He's poison-mean himself and he carries a sawed-off shotgun most of the time. Plays a good hand of draw, they say.

"Four, five outlaws hang out there all the time, but right now there's better than twenty. Tough galoots, too."

"Lefty Hale's down there," Milligan offered. "From the Big Bend country."

"I know him," Hoppy said. "He was one of that outfit from Talley Mountain."

Tex Milligan's eyes brightened. "You know that country? I was born below Shafter, at a place called Burnt Camp."

"I know the place," Hopalong said, smiling. "It's near Fresno Canyon."

"That's right." Milligan grinned. "Well, what do you know?"

Hopalong rinsed out his cup and got to his feet. "We'd better slope it. You patrollin' this line, Kid?"

"Yeah." The boy's eyes went to the other hands, who were busy tightening girths and some distance away. "Hoppy," he said suddenly, "I maybe shouldn't tell this, but I figure I ought to. I thought about tellin' the boss, but I was afraid I'd start trouble. Miss Lenny has been meetin' an hombre in Majuba Canyon."

"Well," Hopalong suggested, "I reckon that's her business. We only ride herd on the cows, Kid."

"Yeah." The boy's face flushed. "But this here hombre—well, he's plumb bad, if you ask me. It's that gunman, Clarry Jacks!"

Hopalong Cassidy remembered the handsome, dashing young man from Katie Regan's and understood how Kid Newton must feel. Clarry Jacks might be all right, but all of Hopalong's instincts warned him that he was not.

"I—I heard some talk over to the ranch," Newton volunteered. "The boss don't want her seein' him atall. He said so, some time back. He ordered Jacks off the place. Jacks laughed at him, then went."

Hopalong nodded. "All right, Kid. Keep it under your hat. I'll think it over." Yet as he rode away he remembered that it was none of his business, not any of his business at all. Newton, he imagined, was more than a little infatuated with Lenny Ronson, and it was easy to understand, as was Lenny's interest in Clarry Jacks.

Frenchy and Tex were already in their saddles, and Hopalong swung up. They were two miles along the trail before he spoke. "What about Jacks? Know anything about him?"

"He's bad," Ruyters said quietly. "He killed a man over to Unionville last year . . . deliberately picked the fight. He's killed three other men I know of and a couple I suspect. That partner of his, Dud Leeman, he's just about as mean himself."

The roundup was still several days away, and there was much work to do before they could begin. It was work that had to be done, by all of them. There might be trouble at the roundup itself, but Hopalong looked for little until it was over. Besides, the losses to Rocking R cattle and the gain by other herds would show up strongly then and bring the whole affair into the open. It might well be that something would occur during the roundup that would start trouble and start it fast.

It would be well to be ready for that, and it looked as if a ride to town and a talk to Shorty Montana were in order. From all he had heard, Montana was a fighter, and that was the sort of man they needed right now. Every fighting man they added to the Rocking R outfit meant that much less danger of trouble. Everybody on this range knew that Montana would take no water from anyone, and that in itself would help.

Frenchy and Milligan were good men. How good the others were remained to be seen.

Moreover, the battle had been opened by his facing of Windy Gore and his beating of Gore's rider. At least they now knew that the Rocking R was not a fat sheep in high oats, to be taken when they wanted it. This would not stop the hardiest ones but might cause the rustling to ease off until after the roundup, when it would be less easy than now.

Where Clarry Jacks fitted into the picture, Cassidy could not guess, and he was not the man to interfere in something that was none of his business.

His thoughts returned to the stage holdup, the murder of Jesse Lock, and the killing of Thacker.

Thacker had been a dangerous gunman, he had learned. Where had the man been going? Who had killed him? A man fearless enough to give Thacker his chance with a gun would be a man among few, a man who could be found without too much trouble, for not many would have dared. It could only be a man supremely confident and supremely arrogant. And a man supremely cold-blooded, for it was probable the same man had murdered Jesse Lock.

As they approached the ranch headquarters the others rode on ahead. Cassidy drew up on a rise and rolled a smoke, considering the whole situation. There were too many angles. The Gores and their 3 G outfit, the rustlers of Corn Patch, Clarry Jacks and whatever he was, and the holdup and killing of Jesse Lock.

Did they tie up anywhere at all? That was a question, but it was doubtful. Many western towns had hangers-on like Jacks. Men who lived on little, put up a big front, and lazed around, playing poker and keeping out of work. Sometimes they were on the rustle. And Jacks was supposed to be a gunfighter. He was cold-blooded. Had it been Jacks who killed Thacker and Lock?

"It must be serious to have you thinking so much."

Hopalong turned to face a tall, stately-looking girl who was beautiful, with quiet dignity and charm.

"It is, I reckon," Cassidy said frankly. "You must be Irene Ronson."

"Yes. You were thinking about the ranch? I often come up here to look at it, and I know I'll miss it when I go."

"You're leaving?"

"Only for town. I'm to marry Dr. Marsh in Seven Pines."

"He's a lucky man."

"I sometimes feel like a traitor." She looked off at the surrounding hills. "With all this trouble I'm afraid of what may happen to the ranch."

"We'll save it," Hopalong said quietly. "Your brother's a good man."

Then he told her about the happenings of the afternoon, leaving out only what Kid Newton had told him about Lenny and Clarry Jacks. She listened attentively and nodded from time to time.

"We've all known there would be trouble with the Gores," she said. "Lenny wanted to send Clarry over there, and he volunteered to go. But Bob wouldn't stand for it. And he wouldn't hire Clarry."

Hopalong secretly thought him wise but said nothing. Irene turned on him suddenly. "You've one enemy now," she said quietly. "I hate to say this, but you've an enemy in my sister. Lenny was furious at Bob for hiring you. She's a wonderful girl and I love her very much, but she's headstrong and she has always believed the man to run the ranch was Clarry Jacks."

"But I'm not running it," he objected. "I'm only segundo—in charge of trouble," he added.

"I know, but Leonora doesn't like it one

bit. She feels left out so much, anyway. Bob and I usually see things much alike, but Lenny . . . well, she has her own viewpoint."

There were hoofbeats behind them, and they turned. Her hair flaming in the late sunlight, Lenny Ronson sat her horse, looking at them. Her face was cold and her eyes level. "That's right, Irene, I have. And my viewpoint is that Hopalong Cassidy should never have been hired!"

Her glance chilled as she turned to meet his eyes. "You know what they are saying, don't you? That you killed Jesse Lock! That you held up the stage! That you killed Thacker!" She paused. "They are saying just that, and they've told Ben Lock. He's in town, and he's looking for you! He's going to kill you! And I"—her eyes flashed—"I'm glad of it!"

CHAPTER 4

SHORTY HUNTS
FOR TROUBLE

When Hopalong swung from the saddle, the Nevada Saloon was ablaze with lights. While loosening the girth he studied the street. Supper should be over at Katie's, and the saloons were doing a rushing business. A cool wind from off the mountains had emptied the street of loafers, and he saw but one man, a solitary figure, leaning idly against an awning support in front of a darkened saddle shop. The man wore miner's boots and a nondescript hat.

Hopalong knocked the dust from his hat, remembering the accusations Lenny Ronson had made. Her attitude had changed since the morning he arrived. Had it been because of learning he was to be right-hand man to her brother? Or because of something she had learned from Clarry Jacks at their meeting in Majuba Canyon?

The last seemed most probable, especially as she reported to him what she had heard was being said in Seven Pines.

He scowled unhappily. Were such things really being said? The place to find out was at Katie's.

And Ben Lock was in town looking for him. Had Lock said he would kill him? Or was that just Lenny talking? Or Jacks speaking through her? Ben Lock came of feudal stock, and he might shoot first and ask questions after. Hopalong crossed the street to Katie's, and pushing open the door, he stepped in.

Katie smiled quickly. She was alone in the restaurant.

"Katie," Cassidy asked quickly, "is Ben Lock in town?"

Her face grew serious instantly. "He sure is, Mr. Cassidy, and he wants to talk to you."

"What sort of hombre is he?"

Katie Regan hesitated, then shook her head. "I—I don't know. He's under thirty, good-looking in a sharp, rugged way, and he doesn't smile very much. Jesse almost worshiped him. He was always telling me things Ben had done.

"They were in some feud in Missouri before coming out here. Their father and uncle were both killed, but Ben finished off the other side. They came west together. He works very hard, and he is strictly honest, I think. And he loved his brother."

Hopalong nodded thoughtfully. "Give me some coffee," he said; then, "coffee and pie."

The door opened suddenly, and Hopalong glanced up. The newcomers were Pony Harper and Clarry Jacks. Both men smiled and nodded. "Howdy, Hopalong," said Harper. "It's all over town about you bein' here! I reckon this is the biggest news in months!"

"Bigger than the holdups?" Hopalong asked dryly.

Harper shrugged. "Those holdups are gettin' so they ain't news." He looked sharply at Hopalong. "By the way, we had us an election today and I'm the new mayor. There was some talk of hirin' a town marshal. It come to me that you were just the man for the job. How about it?"

"I've got a job." Hopalong smiled and shook his head. "Thanks just the same."

"But this one will pay twice as much!" Harper protested. "We'll pay a hundred and fifty a month and you split the costs from any arrests with the J.P." He winked. "That there could run into a sizable chunk of money with this town as tough as it is. Mileage, too. Now that's an item. A marshal can pile up a sight of mileage if he wants."

"I've got a job," Hopalong repeated. "Anyway, I'm a rider, not a peace officer."

"Sorry!" Harper seemed irked. "We could have used you."

Hopalong tasted the coffee, then grinned at Katie. "Ma'am," he said, "I sure hope no cowhand marries you off until I leave town! This is the best coffee I've tasted since leavin' Texas!"

The door swung open, and a man walked into the room. He was short and barrel-chested, with a wide jaw and a broken nose. His eyes were blue, but despite the liquor he seemed to be carrying, his expression was not vague. He had big hands and wore two guns swung low and tied down.

"Shorty," Katie said severely, "you're drunk again!"

The man grinned widely and impudently. "Not—yet! My walk's no worse than usual and I can still talk straight. Only"—his eyes drifted to Pony Harper and Clarry Jacks—"only I do smell somethin' funny, somethin' mighty pecoolyar."

Shorty Montana stared at the two men. "I

sure do! I smell polecat. Two polecatsh!" He looked around in mock bewilderment. "Wheresh the other polecatsh?"

Pony Harper's face hardened and his lips thinned. Clarry Jacks looked ugly, and there was a devil in his eyes. Cassidy could guess why Jacks hesitated to make an issue of it. Montana was popular, and a killing by Jacks would be apt to blow the lid off more than one thing right now. As for Harper, he wanted no part of Montana at any time. It was an interesting and revealing picture. Hopalong studied it while drinking his coffee. Shorty at least was not afraid of either of them, for he did not hesitate to bait them, obviously welcoming trouble. And trouble could not profit either of the others.

Shorty leaned his big hands on the table. "I said—wheresh the other polecatsh?"

"Shorty!" Katie Regan spoke sharply now. "Shorty, come over here and drink your coffee! It's getting cold!"

The drunken man hesitated an instant, staring at the other two, then lurched to a seat. Shaking his head, he muttered, "Women! Women! Never leave a man alone! Gettin' so a man can't even have a decent knock-down-and-drag-out fight without a woman buttin' in! Can't even talk to a couple of polecatsh!"

The door closed softly, and Cassidy noticed the two men had gone quietly outside. He heard a murmur of conversation, and it sounded bitter. He grinned at the thought of what was probably being said. At the same time he was wishing he could overhear it. Whatever those two had to say might be interesting. He doubted that Harper really wanted him as town marshal. What Harper or somebody wanted was to have him away from the Rocking R. But who? And why?

Cassidy went to work on the pie and glanced up to see Shorty Montana staring at him. He continued to eat, and when he had finished the pie and his cup was refilled, he looked at Montana in a friendly, good-natured fashion.

The cowhand stared back at Cassidy.

Hopalong said quietly, "Ronson hired me as segundo. In charge of trouble."

"He needs one," Shorty said dryly, all the apparent drunkenness gone from his tone.

"He does," Cassidy agreed. "Seems the Gores are takin' in a lot of territory out thataway."

"The Gores," Shorty said sincerely, "are big enough to do it."

"Met one of them today," Hopalong continued. "Windy. Had some words. What's the name of that hand of his with the bald head?"

"Hank Boucher," Shorty said.

"Made some trouble for himself," Cassidy explained casually. "He's been advised to try a more agreeable climate."

Shorty Montana was staring at Hopalong. "Boucher," he said, "is plumb salty."

"He's freshened up some now," Hopalong replied. "And Windy's got a bug in his ear. All of which," he added, "builds up to a point. I'm goin' to need more hands. I'm goin' to need a few fightin' men. They tell me you like a scrap, and you size up right to me. How about it?"

Montana hesitated. Then slowly he shook his head. "Had a run-in with that old blaze-face who used to ramrod this country," he said, "and swore I'd never work for him or the brand."

"Anybody can change his mind," Hopalong said. "Young Bob knows he's no fighter, but he's in for a fight. I like him. I'm runnin' the fight. I could use you."

Shorty Montana drank his coffee in silence. Finally he said, "Joe Hartley still there? And that Dan Dusark?"

"Still there."

"Then count me out."

"You don't like them?"

Shorty Montana got to his feet. "Hartley I don't know. But sometimes you wonder why

Dusark don't come to town on Saturday nights like the rest. Then wonder where he does go."

Hopalong studied Montana curiously, knowing that he wanted this man, knowing from what he saw, to say nothing of what he had heard, that this man would be worth a half dozen in a scrap. "Where does he go?"

Montana smiled. "Why, he takes a ride. A long ride. Now you ask yourself where he goes and for what. When you get the answer, maybe you'll know why we don't get along so well."

Shorty Montana went out the door and closed it after him. Hopalong smoked thoughtfully, and then he said, "A good man, that. I'd like to have him."

"You'll get him." Katie was positive. "Leave it to me—and to Shorty himself. He can't stay out of a scrap, and I know he's fairly crazy to be in this one. Then"—she glanced at Hopalong appraisingly—"he likes you."

"Me?" Hopalong looked around in surprise.

"You. I know Shorty. He'll be out nosing around now to find out what happened today between Windy Gore and you. If he likes what he hears, he'll be out to the Rocking R reporting for work. When he comes—and I'll bet you an apple pie against a dollar that he does—just take it for granted and ask no questions."

Hopalong walked outside and studied the street. The man who had stood in front of the harness shop now stood across the street and a short distance up. He was leaning against the wall of a building, only his legs visible.

Hopalong waited an instant, then turned and sauntered slowly down the street, taking his time. Without glancing around, he knew he was being followed. If the man had wished to take a shot at him, there had been several good chances; therefore, either the fellow wished to do some talking or else he was waiting until Hopalong got off the street before he tried shooting. Maybe that was it. Maybe the fellow just wanted a better chance to get away unseen.

Thinking of that, Hopalong kept well into the shadows and took his time considering the situation. Who would want to kill him? There were three possible chances. One of the Gore crowd, one of the holdup men who feared he might know something, or one of the rustler crowd who wanted to keep him out of the picture. Any one of the three was a good bet, but Hopalong was not interested in guessing. He wanted to know.

Pausing on a corner, he drew in a deep breath. His muscles felt alert and ready, and there was rising in him a certain recklessness that he continually fought down. There was that in him that disliked being pushed, and while he knew it might be best to avoid the issue that was presenting itself, he was not the man to do it. He believed in taking the bull by the horns and tail, and this was one time he was going to do it.

That the situation in the Seven Pines country was all set to blow off, he knew. Any action now might start trouble, but he had an idea that the rustlers were lurking around, stealing dribbles of cattle and waiting for the Gores to tangle with the Rocking R in an all-out battle.

Hopalong glanced back once more, then walked on. Stepping off the boardwalk at the end of a building, he turned swiftly into the darkness of an alleyway. He ran a dozen steps, then halted and listened. Behind him he heard boot steps on the boardwalk, then silence. In his mind he could see the unknown follower waiting there, hesitating whether to follow, and probably wondering what Hopalong was up to.

Footsteps sounded on the gravel, and Hopalong knew the man was walking toward him. He scowled thoughtfully, aware that whoever the man was, he was making no effort at concealment. When he was almost abreast of him, Cassidy spoke. "All right, friend, you've come far enough. Huntin' trouble, or just huntin'?"

"Cassidy?"

"Right." Cassidy moved a soundless step left as he spoke, his hands poised above his guns.

"I want to talk. Peaceful talk, but we can't be seen together."

"Lead the way."

The footsteps crunched on down the alley, and Hopalong followed, keeping well to one side. When the man stopped they were in a clump of willows on the edge of town. He turned and faced Hopalong, his hands out away from his sides. "This is peace talk," he repeated. "I'm not honin' for trouble with any of that Bar 20 outfit."

The use of the brand name was something. That meant that the man had probably known or known of Hoppy in the past. "I come to warn you," the man continued. "You're due to walk into a trap if you're not careful."

"Why warn me? Who are you?"

"Carp—from the Butte country."

"Carp?" The name had a familiar sound, but Cassidy could not quite place it.

"Yeah. You and the Bar 20 riders cleaned out the rustlers down in the Butte country after

Nevada and his crowd shot up Johnny Nelson, remember? Well, I was one of 'em."

"I remember. You were the one who sided Tex Ewalt when he was in a tight spot with 'em, and he promised you a break."

"That's right. And what's more, he lived up to his promise and so did you. You stood up and spoke for me at the trial and saved me gettin' my neck stretched. Well, I ain't no better than I used to be, Cassidy, but I know a square shooter when I see one. You see, a few nights ago I was over to Corn Patch and I heard some talk. I heard plans to ambush you and wipe you out.

"Me, I may be a lot of things, but I ain't a dry-gulcher. Nor am I standin' by to see a square man shot down without a chance, not by that bunch of coyotes."

"Thanks, Carp. That's square, and I ain't forgettin' it." Cassidy would have liked to ask the outlaw questions about the holdup or the rustling, but, knowing his man, he knew it would be of no use. Carp had warned him only because of the favor Cassidy had done him before, and also because he was himself a brave man and it went against the grain to see murder done. But that would not allow him to betray his friends or to expose any of their schemes. If the time came when Carp believed it best to talk, he would make up his own mind.

"How's the shootin' planned? You know that?"

"Not exactly, only they'll send word to you that one of your boys is hurt. It'll be in some place where they can lay concealed, and I have an idea, from what was said, it will be over west in the Rosebud Canyon. They'll have seven or eight men all ready to mow you down. They are scared you'll end rustlin' in this country."

"Thanks, Carp." Hopalong hesitated. "What about you?"

Carp chuckled dryly. "Me? I'm splittin' the breeze out of here. I don't mind admittin' I've done a bit of rustlin' myself, but when I heard you was in the country I knew the game was up. I'm headin' for Montana come daybreak."

A tight-riding bunch of horsemen were coming up the street when Hopalong Cassidy reached it, and he faded back against the building for a better look. Standing there in the shadow, he saw five men in the group, and one of the riders was Hank Boucher. Another was Windy Gore.

There was a slight movement across the street, and Hopalong stared hard, straining his eyes to make out the man who was moving among the shadows. Then he saw—it was Shorty Montana.

The puncher was moving after the Gores and following them into the High-Grade Saloon. Hopalong hesitated, then crossed the street and circled for the rear of the saloon.

The High-Grade was more than a saloon, for it was also the town's principal hotel. A two-story frame structure, it housed the bar with its gaming tables, and at the back of the room a stairway led to a narrow balcony. Along the balcony were curtained booths, but in the rear were the hotel rooms, some thirty of them, all small and each one equipped with a wooden bed. There was also a rear stairway to the second floor and a rear door to the first floor.

Cassidy went up the rear stairway to the second floor and tiptoed along the hall to the balcony. Without attracting attention he managed to get into the first booth. There he drew the curtain, leaving it open just enough to enable him to watch the room without being seen.

The Gore outfit was already in the saloon and lined up along the bar. Windy, tall and slack-jawed, Cassidy recognized at once. John he soon picked out by hearing him named, a burly man with thick shoulders and chest who wore a huge reddish mustache and had small, cruel eyes. Con was just as big, but he had none of the bulkiness that his brother showed. He was square-shouldered and muscular, his face clean-shaven and brutally boned. All three men looked tough and all three wore two guns each.

Aside from Hank Boucher, his face bruised and swollen, Cassidy recognized none of them. Shorty Montana had come in and was now walking slowly past them. As he drew abreast of Boucher, he deliberately stopped and eyed his bruised face. Boucher turned, anger mounting within him.

"What's eatin' you?" he demanded.

"Nothin'." Montana had his thumbs tucked behind his belt, and he was elaborately serious. "Just sort of wonderin'."

"About what?" Boucher demanded suspiciously.

Shorty smiled innocently. "I was wonderin' what sort of animal could step on a man's face to make it look so messed up. Now if you were dragged by a horse, it would be more skinned and scratched-like."

"Shut up!" Boucher growled furiously. "Ain't none of your business!"

"That's sure the truth," Montana agreed pleasantly. "It's none of my business. On the other hand, can't a man express a friendly sort of interest? Can't blame a body for bein' curious, can you? I knew an hombre down to Tombstone who got him a face like that, but he was kicked by a mule.

"Now that there eye," Shorty continued, "it's cut pretty deep. That might've been kicked by a mule, all right. And your mouth there, lips all puffed and swollen—don't reckon that could be—"

"Shut up!" Boucher turned on Montana. "Shut up or I'll do it for you!"

Shorty Montana backed off two steps in mock fear. "Hey! What's the matter? I ain't huntin' trouble, Boucher! Just sort of wonderin' what happened."

"You've wondered enough!" Pony Harper spoke abruptly from the end of the bar. "We want no trouble in here, Montana. I won't stand for it!"

"Aw, cut it out, Pony!" Montana objected, grinning. "I was just a-funnin', that's all! Why, I come in to say goodby to the 3 G boys, seein' as they are leavin' the country."

Conversation stilled and all ears were listening. "Leavin'?" Harper was startled. He stared at John Gore. "You boys pullin' your freight?"

"No!" Gore exploded, astonished and angry. "Where'd you get a fool idea like that, Shorty?"

"Why, I heard Hopalong Cassidy was fighting segundo out at the Rockin' R now, so I figured you boys would be splittin' the breeze out of here almost any time. I didn't reckon," he said seriously, "you'd be so plumb foolish as to stay around and buck him!"

"Well, of all the gall!" John Gore slammed his glass on the bar. "When we pull out for any overrated gunfighter like him, you'll know it, Shorty! We're here to stay, and believe me, we'll stay, Hopalong Cassidy or not!"

Shorty nodded agreeably. "I'm settin' 'em up, Slim," he said to the bartender. "Drinks for the whole 3 G outfit on me!" He slammed a gold piece on the bar and waited while the bartender filled their glasses, then lifted his own. "To the 3 G outfit! A bunch that was game enough to stand their ground and die in their boots!"

Pent-up rage spluttered from Windy Gore's lips and he turned. "You think that's funny, Montana?" He glared. "I've got a good notion to take you apart right now and see what makes you tick!"

"Don't try it, Windy!" Montana warned, his voice ringing with sudden sincerity. "You haven't got what it takes! Besides"—he grinned suddenly—"Mr. Harper wouldn't like it. He sure does hate to get blood on his floor."

John Gore was no fool. He was shrewd enough to know that a statement of purpose made now would be remembered by many of the listeners in the days to come, and he knew also that public opinion was important.

"We aren't lookin' for trouble," he said, phrasing his words with care. "It's true that we are runnin' cows on range relinquished by the Rockin' R, and as long as the grazing between the Blues and the Antelopes has been abandoned I see nothing wrong with it."

This was untrue and he knew it, yet he also knew that few of the bystanders had ever actually ridden over that range since the death of Cattle Bob. They would be in no position to dispute his statement. He had made his own plans, and the arrival of Hopalong Cassidy might complicate things but would be allowed to change nothing. He wanted the Rocking R range for himself and intended to have it. He was a domineering man but far from a fool. He was ready and able to use force—not the thoughtless, sometimes reckless force Windy might use or the brutality of Con, but force. Hard, driving force that would take him at once to a victory.

"Free range," he continued, "is only held by an outfit so long as they keep it stocked."

Hopalong Cassidy had moved from his

curtained booth and had come most of the way down the steps without attracting attention. All eyes had been centered on Montana and the Gore outfit. Now he spoke.

"You're mistaken," he said quietly. "The Rockin' R has relinquished nothing at all. Our cattle still run on that range, and they will continue to do so. Furthermore, you have been ordered to drive your cattle the other side of the Blues. I repeat that order now."

For an instant there was silence. John Gore was inwardly furious. Better than any of the others, he saw how Cassidy had turned the tables on him. Now any action of his that led to violence would certainly be considered his fault. He fixed his eyes on the bar, stared at it bitterly. Then, feeling eyes upon him, he looked around to meet the gaze of Pony Harper. He saw the slight inclination of Harper's eyes toward the office of the hotel and frowned slightly.

There had never been anything but a speaking acquaintance between himself and Harper. He did not like the man and saw no more reason for beginning to like him now. However, there was something in the gesture that interested him. After a moment or two he turned and started down the room toward the door. As he walked he did not feel another pair of cold blue eyes following him. Hopalong Cassidy had seen the gesture. What lay behind it he did not know, but it could scarcely mean anything except trouble for himself.

Shorty Montana moved up beside him. "Looks like you hired yourself a hand, Cassidy," he said. "All right if I show up in the mornin'?"

"You just know it is!" Hopalong said emphatically.

Montana said, "You know, of course, you were just talkin' through your hat like Gore was? There isn't goin' to be any peace in this valley until that Gore outfit's wiped out! And some more I've a hunch I could put a name to!"

"You're right, I'm thinkin'." Hopalong stared at him thoughtfully. "Reckon I've a little ridin' to do."

Shorty hesitated. "Hoppy," he said seriously, "this don't make any promises for me, does it, about that Dusark? I don't cotton to that hombre."

"It makes no promises," Cassidy agreed. "Only take it easy. Don't push either him or Hartley."

Cassidy turned to leave the room, and Montana followed him. "If I'm not at the ranch in the mornin'," Cassidy said, "you tell Bob

Ronson I hired you, and go to work. You know what needs to be done on a cow outfit."

"Where you goin'?" Montana demanded.

Hopalong hesitated. "Why, I reckon to Corn Patch. I think I'll just take a pasear over there and see what goes on."

Montana shook his head. "Hoppy, you watch yourself. That bunch is poison. And don't you trust that Poker Harris—not by a jugful! He'd kill a man as quick as he'd fry an egg!"

CHAPTER 5

EXTRA ACES

Poker Harris had been the guiding hand at Corn Patch for more years than even the oldest other inhabitant could remember. His background was unknown, except that it seemed more than probable that it had included a postgraduate course in the unrefined arts of murder, mayhem, and assorted varieties of robbery.

Six feet and four inches in his sockless feet, Poker Harris was two hundred and sixty pounds of bone and muscle overlaid with a deceptive veneer of fat. His jowls were heavy, usually unshaven and flushed, and his lashless eyes peered from between folds of loose flesh. His hands were large, very thick and powerful, covered with reddish hair. His head was partially bald, and he made up for that lack of hirsute adornment by a surplus on his chest.

Customarily he wore a six-shooter tucked behind the rope that did duty as a belt, but his favorite weapon, which he was almost never without, was a sawed-off shotgun fitted with a homemade pistol grip. It was this weapon, as much as anything else, that terrorized those close to him, for many a man will face a pistol with equanimity and yet shrink from the blasting of a shotgun at close range.

A drifting miner some fifty years before, when prospectors in the region were extremely rare, had found a patch of corn growing on a flatland alongside a water hole. Evidently someone had planted this corn, cultivated it for a time, and then gone on about his business, or perhaps had died in the back country. Given a chance, the corn made good and grew rapidly; unharvested, it scattered its kernels about, and more corn had grown.

Attracted by its presence, the miner had built a shack. He found some placer gold in a nearby wash, picked up a couple of cows lost by a wagon train, and soon found himself settled in an easy way of life. Other miners came, lived for a time, abandoned their shacks and diggings, then moved on. Then there was a brief boom during which a saloon was thrown together and a bunkhouse that passed as a hotel was built. The shacks exchanged owners nightly, weekly, or monthly, and without title beyond that of possession. Then Poker Harris came and stayed.

The original inhabitant disappeared, and ownership of the cows, now grown to a herd of an even dozen, was transferred to Harris. By use of appropriate gestures with the shotgun, Harris acquired title to the saloon and the shacks. He designated sleeping quarters as he wished, and if any sought to dispute possession they had a choice of leaving town fast or being assigned a permanent residence on Boot Hill.

Some of this Hopalong Cassidy knew. Much he had yet to find out. What Poker Harris knew he kept to himself, and what his dealings were with those who came and went around Corn Patch he kept a secret. Like many pioneers of both good and bad vintage, Harris had a fine memory for names, faces, and descriptions. Newspapers were sadly lacking, but word-of-mouth descriptions were correspondingly accurate. Few men appeared at Corn Patch whose backgrounds were unknown to Poker Harris.

Corn Patch itself lay in a canyon once called Eldorado by some optimist or humorist. A mountain ridge that towered nearly five thousand steep feet above the town divided it from the mining town of Unionville, some five miles south, and the immediate canyon in which Corn Patch lay was steep-sided and the sides lined with shacks. From his windows Poker Harris could see most of those shacks and watch the comings and goings of the inhabitants. Consequently he was his own espionage service, and little took place within the confines of the town that he did not know.

The saloon, which was also his office and home, was a stone-and-frame structure, badly weathered and never painted. It backed up against the southeast wall of the canyon and looked right down the main and only street, which was also the canyon's bottom. A store, the bunkhouse, a blacksmith shop, and a scattering of shacks completed the street, all easily seen from the stool where Poker usually sat.

Behind him was a rack containing a Sharps .50, a Spencer .56, a Winchester .44, and two shotguns other than the sawed-off he usually carried. These were always loaded, the rack was locked, and he carried the only key. Under the bar, within grasp of his hand, was another Spencer .56, a weapon whose ventilating possibilities were scarcely exceeded by an artillery piece. In short, Poker Harris was monarch of all he surveyed and intended to remain so—against any one man or any gang of men.

Both attempts had been made. The first

had been tried four times, accounting for four of the graves on his private Boot Hill, and the last had been tried twice, accounting for seven more graves. At least four other graves were filled by itinerants who seemed doubtful to Poker, who settled his doubts with lead.

A dozen men idled about the saloon playing desultory poker. Harris dozed at the bar. It was during one of the intervals of wakefulness that he glanced past the bottom of his stein to see a rider turn into the trail that doubled as street. The rider was astride a white gelding that walked fast and smoothly. The rider himself wore a black wide-brimmed hat. He had a tanned, pleasant countenance, worn black trousers tucked into cowboy boots, and two white-handled, tied-down guns. He also wore a black vest.

It was the Winchester in the saddle boot that did not click in the brain of Poker Harris. Had it been a Sharps, he would at once have thought of Hopalong Cassidy. As it was, he did not know that Hoppy had at last yielded, temporarily at least, to the arguments of his old Bar 20 comrade Red Connors. The rifle argument between the two had gone on for years, and Connors, a wizard with the weapon, had at last prevailed upon his friend. That he had won a victory he did not know, and if Red Connors had appeared on the horizon, Hoppy would hastily have concealed the Winchester and resorted to his old and well-loved buffalo gun.

Poker Harris linked men up to things, and the love of Cassidy for the Sharps was known wherever there were cow camps or men from the cattle drives. The bone-handled Colts he recognized instantly as belonging to a man who understood their use, but this man had come to Corn Patch, a place of safety to outlaws and of death to officers of the law. Therefore, this man must be an outlaw. Still, Poker Harris was wary.

Pushing open the door, Cassidy entered the long room. Men glanced up, then went on with whatever they were doing. Harris would take care of things. He always did. No sense being too efficient.

"Water," Hopalong suggested, and Harris swept a thick hand to the back bar for a glass, filled it, and shoved it toward Hopalong. Hopalong tasted the water, then drank it all. "Good," he said.

"Spring water," Harris replied with pardonable pride. "No alkali."

Poker Harris liked a man who had little to say. The cold blue eyes measured him. Harris felt a moment of uneasiness and that disturbed him, for so superb was his confidence that he was rarely uneasy about anything.

Cassidy glanced at the men playing poker. "Any draw players around?"

Harris's eyes flickered. "Few. I play a few hands occasionally."

"Like it myself," Hopalong agreed, "if the players aren't too stuffy. I like a fast game," he added, "where a man takes care of hisself."

Harris shifted on his stool, warming toward this hard-eyed stranger. "I'll break out a new deck." He glanced out the window. "Better put your horse up. Hot out there."

Turning, Hopalong walked from the saloon, and Poker Harris stared after him, watching the choppy walk, the sloping shoulders. This was a man he should know. He shook his head with disgust. It would come to him. He smiled when the man swung into the saddle instead of merely leading his horse across the street. It was typical of a rider.

The livery stable was long, wide, and cool inside. The old familiar barn smells and sounds made Hopalong smile. They were smells he would always love and sounds he knew. The blowing of a horse, the drone of flies hovering in the shadows, the occasional stamp of a hoof on soft earth and hay. He led the white gelding into a stall and stripped off the saddle and bridle, giving the horse a quick going-over with a handful of hay. Digging around, he found a corn bin and poured a quart of corn into a small feed box in the stall. Then he stepped to the door and, keeping in the shadow and out of the sun, lit a match.

That he was on dangerous ground he well knew. Poker Harris was a man who would kill and had killed on the slightest provocation. If he got so much as an idea who his new guest was, he might shoot without comment or accusation—and he might not. He was supremely confident, with just reason, in Corn Patch.

Hopalong strolled aimlessly down the line between the two rows of stalls checking each, wondering if he would find a horse with a blaze on its face and side . . . the horse that he had seen among the riders heading toward the hold up. He quickly ascertained that no such horse was among those present. There might be other barns in town, or a hideout in the hills where horses could be kept. He turned and walked back across the sun-baked street toward the saloon.

Harris looked around at him. "Well, how about that game? Interested?"

"Sure am! Blind openers?"

"My game too." Poker heaved himself from his stool and ambled around the bar to an empty table. He dropped into a huge chair, obviously built for his own comfort, then turned slightly. "Any you boys want in?"

A surly-eyed black-haired man looked up. "Not with you, I don't! Your game's too fast for my blood!"

Poker Harris chuckled. "Plays a careful game, that one."

A narrow-faced man with a petulant, irritable mouth sauntered over. "Name's Troy. I'll sit in."

Two others, a burly cowpuncher named Hankins, with broken, dirty nails and quick, hard eyes, and a tall, gray-haired man with dark eyes and smooth hands. "Blind openers?" The gray-haired man smiled. "That can be rough."

Harris jerked a thumb toward the man. "Name's Drennan. Yours?"

"Red River Regan." Cassidy smiled.

"Cut high for deal?" Harris asked casually. He glanced around the table, not to find if his suggestion was agreeable, but rather to place all his men and fix their positions in his memory. Red River Regan appeared to have a roll, and he was slated for a cleaning. Suckers had been all too scarce lately.

"High or low, either one." Cassidy leaned back in his chair, apparently uninterested in the swiftly moving fingers of the saloonkeeper, who was shuffling the cards a bit. He shoved them toward Cassidy, who cut an eight. Drennan cut a six, Hankins and Troy both cut tens, and Poker Harris a king.

Harris shuffled the cards once more, slapped them down before Troy, who cut, and then he dealt. The game moved quietly along, and Hopalong found himself winning a few small pots. Drennan won, and Harris. Both Troy and Hankins were losers, with Troy growling at his ill luck. Hopalong's own very real ability with cards had been tapered to a fine point under the masterly training of Tex Ewalt, poker player extraordinary, and what Tex did not know, nobody knew. Recognizing at once that Harris, while handy with cards, was no Ewalt, Cassidy proceeded to play carefully and wait for a showdown. It came suddenly.

Both Drennan and Hankins had dropped out. Harris, Troy, and Hopalong had stayed. Harris mopped his sweaty face with a handkerchief and stared at his cards, lifting his eyes in a casual glance across the table at Troy. As he did so his left thumb projected from the fist of his clenched left hand.

Hopalong caught the gesture from the tail

of his eye and grinned inwardly. So this was it? They were going to keep raising? All right, he would stay with them. He glanced once more at his full house, queens and sixes. Harris shoved three blue chips into the center of the table. "Raise it thirty."

Hankins stared at Troy, then looked at Hopalong. Troy licked his lips. "See you, and up ten."

Hopalong studied his stack of chips and tossed four blues to the center. "Call," he said quietly.

His quick eye had caught a surreptitious signal from Harris to Troy. "Four kings," Harris said coolly, and slapped his stacked cards on the table, only the top card showing.

Troy's right hand shot out instantly to spread them, and Hopalong's left was faster. Before Troy's hand could reach the cards, his own was there. He spread the hand with a swift gesture. Only four cards showed—and only three kings.

Troy's face turned ugly, and Poker Harris's eyes tightened. Hopalong only grinned. "You must have dropped one, Harris. I only see three kings."

Harris craned his neck to see under the table, then ducked quickly and came up with a card. It was a trey. His face was red. "Mistake," he said. "I'd have sworn I had four kings."

Cassidy shrugged. "Forget it. We all make mistakes. Looks," he added innocently, "like my full house takes the pot?"

Troy had withdrawn his hand, and Cassidy coolly swept the chips toward him. That fourth king had been in Troy's hand, and had he spread the cards, he would have added it to those already there. It was an old trick, and one Ewalt had showed Cassidy in a bunkhouse years before.

It was Hopalong's deal, and he gathered the cards clumsily toward him. He had already noted two aces among the discard, and he neatly swept them into a bottom stock as he gathered the cards together.

He riffled the cards, spotted another ace and, in a couple of passes in shuffling, added it to his bottom stock. Palming the three, he passed the deck to Harris for cutting, returned them to the bottom after the cut, and calmly dealt five hands, giving himself two of the aces in bottom deals.

Drennan promptly glanced at his cards and tossed them aside. Hankins stayed and tossed in a red chip. Troy upped it five, and then Poker Harris grinned over at Hopalong.

"Reckon we'll see how you like it, Red! I'll see that ten and lift her forty!"

Cassidy hesitated, studied his cards, then raised twenty more. Hankins folded and Troy raised, Harris raised again, and they made another round of the table. At the draw Harris took two cards and Troy and Cassidy three each. One of the three Hoppy dealt himself was the remaining ace from his bottom stock.

Troy promptly tossed two blue chips into the pot. Harris saw him and raised, and Hopalong sat back in his chair and grinned at them. His hard blue eyes were smiling over the ice that glinted in their depths. Drennan suddenly shifted his feet and looked anxiously at Poker Harris, but the big man was looking at Hopalong. Hankins sat silent, his big hands resting on the arms of his chair. Troy twisted nervously and glared at Hopalong for the delay.

Hankins's guns, Hopalong noted, were almost under the arms of his chair, which precluded a swift draw. Drennan wore no gun in sight, and it was a question whether he would declare himself in or not. If trouble showed, Troy would be the first to move. He was the sort to go off half-cocked. Harris was the tough one.

"Let's make it pot limit," Cassidy said, chuckling. "I like 'em bloody!"

Troy swore bitterly as Harris nodded assent, then threw in his hand and drew back slightly, leaving himself in position to cover Hopalong if trouble started.

Poker Harris studied the man across the table with ill-concealed curiosity. It was possible the man who called himself Red River Regan might have guessed their play on the last hand. If he had guessed it, he knew something about crooked cards. If it had been mere chance that his hand had beaten Troy to the spread, he might be just a lucky cowhand. While inclining to this view, Harris was uncertain, and uncertainty he definitely did not like. He did not like it in others, and he liked it even less in himself.

"Pot limit," he said, "can run into money. You got it?"

For answer Hopalong drew a thick roll of bills from his pocket and placed them beside his chips. "I'll cover any play you make, Harris," he said carelessly. "Make her as tough as you like."

"Lot of money for a cowhand," Harris suggested.

"I make good money." Hopalong grinned widely.

This Red River Regan had dealt the cards, but his handling of them had been clumsy, and if he was a gambler, he looked less like one than any man Harris had ever seen. So far he had played a fair game of draw, but nothing unusual. It was true that twice, when Harris had planned a kill, Cassidy had thrown in his hand and passed.

"No," Harris said, "no pot limit, but I'll bet you a flat five hundred over what's in the pot now that I got you beat."

"Call," Hopalong said, still smiling. He spread his cards as he spoke—four aces. Three by bottom dealing and one by accident.

Poker Harris's eyes bulged. He came half out of his chair, the cords in his neck swelling. "Why, you mangy wolf!"

Troy's grab for a gun was wasted. With a swift motion Hopalong had sprung back, knocking over his chair as his Colts leaped to his hands.

Troy's hand froze, and Harris stiffened where he stood. Cassidy smiled. "What's the matter? You got aces too?" He motioned with his guns. "Back up!"

Holstering his left-hand gun, he turned over Harris's hand, then chuckled. "Your aces came from a newer deck, Poker. You should use two decks equal so it won't show up." Calmly he began to pocket the money. "Sorry to spoil this game for you boys, but you started playin' rough. I just kept it up." He nodded toward his hand. "Four bullets. Don't make me use any more."

Troy was livid with fury, Poker Harris big, utterly contained, only his eyes showing the rage that consumed him. Hankins, whose hands had dropped only to realize the futility of attempting a draw from his position, held his place. Only Drennan seemed unmoved and somewhat curious.

"Enjoyed the game," Hopalong said quietly. "Now you boys sit quiet while I leave."

"Wait a minute!" Harris had relaxed in his chair. "Why leave? Strikes me you're an hombre knows his way around. You handle your guns faster than any man I ever saw—except one. Want a job?"

Hopalong gestured at the money. "With all that? You crazy?"

"That's chicken feed. There's plenty around here."

"Boss—" Troy started to protest.

"Shut up!" Harris replied irritably. "I can use a man like you."

Red River Regan shrugged. "I'll always talk business."

"Then find yourself a bunk over there. No hard feelin's. Stick around until mornin' and we'll make medicine."

"Sure." Hopalong coolly holstered his gun.

Troy's eyes were ugly. "I'll kill you!" he said. "You don't size up right to me!"

"Any time you're ready," Cassidy said quietly, "just go to it!"

Troy's hands were trembling on the verge of a draw, and Hopalong knew it. He had seen such men, men driven by such a lust to kill that nothing mattered.

"Troy!" Harris swore at him. "Don't be a blame fool! Cut it out!"

Troy spat viciously, then wheeled and walked from the room. Cassidy stared after him, then shrugged. But his face was thoughtful.

Hopalong suspected that neither he nor his money would make it through the night, and now he wanted nothing so much as to get away . . . but without trouble. He turned to Harris. "See you tomorrow, then," he said. "I'll see my horse is all right, then turn in."

When he went out the door he faded abruptly to the right and into the shadows. Someone was moving in the livery-stable door, but it was not Troy. Dropping from the porch in front of the saloon, he hiked across the street. A big man passed him almost in the door, a man who looked very familiar. Hopalong did not see the man turn to stare after him, but went into the stall and hurriedly slapped the saddle on the white gelding, then the bridle.

He walked the horse to the door and had him there as the big man turned to go into the saloon. That big man had stopped for several minutes on the steps, looking back, trying to make up his mind whether he had been recognized or not. At this stage of the game Dan Dusark did not want to be recognized. He opened the door and walked in.

"Howdy, Harris," he said, shoving his hat back on his head. He looked at Poker Harris. "What was he doin' here?" He jerked his head in the direction of the livery stable.

"Why, you know him?" Harris stared hard at Dusark.

"Know him?" Dusark exploded. "Of course I know him! That's the new segundo on the Rockin' R. That's Hopalong Cassidy."

"What!" Poker Harris's face went livid, then a dark fury of blood. "Did you say Hopalong Cassidy?"

Hankins swore and grabbed for his guns. Two other men went out of the door behind him, and Harris jerked a shotgun from under the bar. They rushed to the bunkhouse, and only their own men snored there. They rushed to the stable, but the white horse was gone!

Harris shouted and raved, but Dusark lighted a smoke. "No use to get excited," he said calmly. "He's gone, and if you know anythin' about him you couldn't find him out there tonight with a search warrant, believe you me!"

Walking his horse down the canyon while Dusark was talking to Harris, Hopalong swung into the saddle and rode swiftly out into the valley below. He did not turn northwest toward the Rockin' R, but southwest toward the stagecoach route. It was as good a time as any to look around the scene of the holdup. His visit to Corn Patch had netted him little beyond his winnings, yet he did know the sort of men to be found there and what might be expected of them.

Poker Harris was shrewd, capable, and dangerous. Troy was vicious as a sidewinder, erratic, and not to be trusted under any circumstances, but he was also a man whose own viciousness would defeat him. Hankins was tough —next to Harris the toughest of the lot. And Drennan—Drennan was an uncertainty. Of the others who had been around he knew little beyond what their presence in the place indicated. They were outlaws, drifters, cowhands gone bad, and the raw material of hell in the borning.

If the three moving forces in the Seven Pines country were tied together, there was as yet no indication of it that he could see. The Gores wanted the Rockin' R range, the rustlers wanted cattle, and the gang that pulled the stage holdup wanted—and had—gold.

There was no uncertainty about the 3 G outfit. The Gore boys had a goal in mind and would waste no time in achieving it, nor would they hesitate to throw lead. The rustlers no doubt had a tie-up with Harris. The holdup men, whoever they might be, would have to have a tighter organization than such a man as Harris could handle. Their greatest problem would be disposal of the gold itself, and raw gold in quantity presented a very real problem in the marketing.

Dark as it soon became, Hopalong had no trouble holding to his direction. Without landmarks from this approach, he nevertheless had the stars to guide him on a course, and knew that if he headed in his present direction he must sooner or later run into the stage trail. Heading south, he made camp in a small hollow among the hills near Poker Gap.

Fixing coffee and a quick meal, Hopalong

then killed his fire and, moving back into the sage a short distance, spread his sugan and rolled up.

Silence awakened Cassidy. Total, complete silence. The pulsing of the crickets had stilled; no wind, no movement of small animals in the brush. It was as if the entire landscape had frozen in fear. Even the breeze was holding its breath. Hopalong's right hand closed on the grip of one of his pistols, and he slowly turned his head to look across the campsite at Topper. In the dark the big gelding was only a pale blur, but Hoppy could tell his head was up and his ears pricked, focused intently on something in the distance. A glance at the sky told him that it was near three o'clock.

Taking a fresh grip on the gun, he rolled out of bed, eyes scanning the darkness. Nothing moved; the night waited, tense in anticipation. He was just considering putting the Colt aside to pull on his boots when there was a sound from far off. It was like distant thunder in a narrow valley, like blasting powder set off deep in a mine, like a huge boulder rolling down a steep hillside; getting closer and closer. . . .

The earth under Hopalong's bare feet trembled, then jerked. Topper snorted, prancing backward. A rock fell, off to his right, hit with a clatter, and then all was still. After a moment or two the silence was broken by the plaintive call of a night bird, then the sound of a single cricket, but soon it was joined by others. Topper blew, and Hopalong went over to comfort him.

"Easy, boy. Just an earthquake, that's all. Take it easy an' we'll see if we can't sleep for a couple more hours."

At the first gray light he was out of bed and building a fire in a small hollow where the flame would be concealed. He used dry sticks and knew they would allow almost no smoke. All the while he kept a sharp lookout on the country around him, watching for any sign of movement or smoke.

The events of last night had focused Hopalong's thinking on caution. That he was in the enemy's country he knew, and the holdup gang might have their hideout anywhere in the area. From now on he would have to exercise utmost care. Swinging into the saddle, he moved out, keeping to washes and bottoms, avoiding all ridge lines and hills. As he rode, his attention was divided between the country itself and the ground beneath.

Suddenly he drew up. A fresh line of

tracks, probably only hours old, crossed before him, and one of the hoofmarks had that same close-trimmed look as one of the horses ridden in the holdup! This was luck! Hopalong studied that track, as well as the three accompanying it, for in the future he might not be so fortunate as to see that one print. However, the other forefoot was also closely trimmed, and the horse toed in slightly.

From under the big hat Hopalong scanned the country. His cold blue eyes left nothing unseen. They were eyes long accustomed to searching desert and range, and he knew how to look for what he saw. His eye would instantly separate anything from the surrounding terrain that did not belong there. When his inspection was completed he started on, but he did not deliberately follow the trail of the horse. He headed in the same direction, swinging on ahead to cut the trail at another point.

Before him the sandy knolls of the desert, covered with sagebrush mingled with creosote, rolled back in a wide but narrowing fold. Huge plates of rock pushed up, the strata in them visibly tilted toward the sky. Here was a piece of the fault along which had run last night's minor earthquake. The trail he followed headed into the gap between those tilted rocks.

He studied it with care, then turned Topper and rode up the side of the hill across from the trail. Keeping below the line of sight from beyond the ridge, he pushed on for half a mile and halted. Leaving the gelding in the juniper, he made his way to the crest and, removing his hat, peered over the top.

The space between had narrowed into a rocky defile, and he could vaguely make out what seemed to be the trail below him. Turning his eyes, he could see up the defile through a maze of gigantic ledges into what seemed to be a canyon, but this was no canyon worn by the slow hand of time, but rather an enormous crack caused by some not-too-ancient upheaval of the earth. Red and raw, the ledges exposed the broken fangs of their ugly jaws to the morning sky, and between two of them lay a narrow valley, in the bottom of which were several makeshift shelters of stone, adobe, and logs. In a pole corral were three horses, and the whiter marks of a trail led away even deeper into the maze of faulted rock.

As Hopalong watched, a man came to the door of one of these shelters and threw a bucket of water onto the ground. Then he walked out of sight behind some rock. When he next appeared, the bucket was full. He went back into the cabin.

For an hour Hopalong carefully studied the situation. Several times he shifted his position for a different viewpoint. To approach up the usual path through the rocks looked to be foolhardy in the extreme, for these men would be taking no chances, and the sight of a stranger would be enough to start them shooting. Yet no matter how he studied the terrain, he could not see what became of the path that vanished into the rocks.

Returning to his horse, he mounted and started riding west. The trail was precarious and he worked his way in and around the tangle of canyons and washes, trying to get at the upper end of the valley to see where the trail he had glimpsed would emerge. Some bygone earthquake had created havoc with the country, and so it was not as easy to read the terrain as it was in a country of natural grades.

Emerging from the tangle, he found himself below the crest of a long ridge. Turning in the saddle, he could see that a high peak ended the ridge, and beyond were two more peaks. The canyon he was looking for must lie between those peaks and this ridge.

Mopping the sweat from his face, for the morning was already warm, Hopalong studied the situation once more but saw nothing new.

Following a vague hunch, he pushed on into a tangle of juniper, where the ground seemed to slant sharply away, and found himself at the head of a steep declivity, a rock slide that slanted sharply away for at least two hundred yards, then disappeared out of sight around a shoulder.

Dismounting, Hoppy worked his way slowly down the slope, leaving Topper tied at the top. When he reached the shoulder, he saw that the slide made a ramp that changed directions but fell sharply away to the bottom of a canyon that could only be the one he had glimpsed. If such was the case, it extended much farther than he had believed. Returning for Topper, Hopalong led the horse carefully down over the rocks. An excellent mountain horse, the gelding took it with patience and some prick-eared interest. Reaching the trail, Hopalong saw nothing behind him in the direction of the small cluster of huts, but before him, in a small amphitheater in the mountains, lay a forest of pine and fir, and in the back of the hollow was the stone face of a building.

Working his way into the basin, Hopalong studied the building. It was a rebuilt cliff dwelling that had obviously been found in good shape. Nearby was a corral, and five beautiful horses stood in it. Hoppy could hear water running, and there appeared to be plenty of grass. He took another step, then stopped abruptly. One of the horses in the corral was that same white-splashed paint horse he had seen in the holdup bunch!

CHAPTER 6

FRAZER MAKES
AN ERROR

Duck Bale was mad. He was mad clean through. For three days before the last holdup and now for every day since then he had been stuck at the hideout, and Duck was a man who liked company.

Frazer was here, of course, but nobody ever claimed that Bud Frazer was good company. He slept most of the time, growled about doing his share of the work, and played solitaire the rest of the time. Duck was a man who liked to talk, and on occasion he liked to listen. Mostly it was just that he liked to talk himself, which was one reason he had the nickname. The other reason was his long nose and flappy lips.

He was good and mad this morning. Frazer had crawled out of bed long enough to eat and had then gone back. He was lying there now, snoring like all get-out. Why wasn't Laramie here? Now Laramie was all right, a pleasant man, but a fighter too. Duck Bale had his own ideas about fighters, and in his mind Laramie stacked up as the toughest of the lot. He was slick with a six-gun and a handy man with a rifle. Someday Laramie would tangle with the boss; Bale was sure of that. He had been pretty sore when the news reached them of how Jesse Lock had been killed.

"It's not decent," he complained to Duck on the quiet. "Lock was a good man and tried to make a fight of it. It wasn't right to kill him thataway."

"Don't let the boss hear you say that," Duck warned. "You know how he is!"

"I sure do," Laramie agreed, his eyes cold.

Duck Bale caught the inflection and admitted to himself that Laramie was right. The boss was cold-blooded. He would shoot a man down without a chance. He wished Laramie was here now. He wanted to tell him about the gold being gone. Maybe it was just that the boss was fixing to get rid of it, but anyway, it had been taken away from the house during the night.

He stared irritably at Bud Frazer. The bald-headed gunman was sprawled on his rum-

pled bunk, snoring peaceably. They had had
another argument that morning with a lot of
loud talk and shouting. Frazer did not like him,
and Frazer was lazy. He had not made his bunk
in four days. Nor had he helped with the
cleanup job—not that they ever did much of it.

Duck walked outside and had started for
the barn when he heard a horse. He turned
instantly, expecting to see either the boss or
Laramie. It was neither. The man on the white
gelding was a stranger, a cold-faced man with
chill blue eyes and sloping shoulders. He drew
up and chuckled. "Name fits all right. You
Duck Bale?"

"Yeah." Duck suddenly realized that his
gun belt was hanging over the back of a chair in
the bunkhouse. "Who are you?"

"Name of Red River Regan." The
stranger slid from his horse and stretched. "He
said you had quite a layout here and you sure
have. I had a time findin' the place."

Duck Bale was in a quandary. Nothing had
been said about any new men, but this fellow
knew his name, seemed to know his way
around, and obviously had known how to get
here. Moreover, he wore those two Colts like
he was used to them. "How did you find it?" he
said.

"Boss told me." He looked around again,

then led his horse into the shade of some trees near the stable and tied him near a patch of grass. "He said there'd be another man here. Bud Something-or-other?"

"Bud Frazer. He's asleep. He's always asleep." There was an irritable tone to Duck's voice, and Hopalong had gauged his man correctly. He suppressed a grin. "You fixin' to feed the horses?"

"Yeah. Bud should've done it, but that hombre's the laziest man I ever did see."

"Got a fork? I'll help. Show me where the hay is."

Duck lit up, then led the way to the stable. Behind it there was a comfortably large stack of hay. In no time at all, hay had been forked to the horses and a bait of corn given each one.

Duck was still suspicious, but the stranger's confidence and easy manner had him puzzled. If the man did not rightly belong, he would never have found his way here in the first place, nor would he be so much at home. Grateful to have somebody to talk to and some help with the work, Bale was not inclined to ask too many questions. In all the time they had used the place nobody had ever appeared who did not belong there.

Hopalong had looked the place over carefully before approaching Duck. He knew he was taking a chance, but he had overheard the extended quarrel that morning and got their names from it and also hints regarding the characters of the two men, as well as the substance of the disagreement between them.

"Eat yet?" Duck inquired suddenly. "I haven't washed up, if you want somethin'. May be some coffee left."

"Sure!" Hopalong drew a deep breath. He knew this could develop into a tight spot if anyone else showed up. If the boss came, whoever he was, Hopalong would truly be out of luck. Or even if the unknown Laramie showed up, for that one might be sharper than Duck Bale. Whatever Cassidy learned would have to be learned fast, for every minute of his stay would increase his danger.

"Quite a place, ain't she?" Duck said, grinning at him. "Boss sure picked him a hideout! Been wonderin' how he knowed it was here, but from the way he acts, he knowed about it for a long time! Plenty long, if you ask me.

"Maybe we aren't the first to use it. Anyway, I've seen a posse ride within a dozen feet of the entrance and miss it.

"Keep a good store of grub on hand, extry horses, and plenty of ammunition. No army could ever take this place."

"Doesn't look it." Hopalong put his cup back on the table. "Must get tiresome stayin' here, though." He spoke innocently, as if he had not heard Duck griping that morning. "He don't look much company." Hoppy indicated the sleeping outlaw. "Me, I'm a friendly sort of person. Like to talk and hear myself spoken to."

Duck warmed immediately. This new-comer was a kindred soul, and it was about time they got somebody in the outfit who acted like a human being. Laramie was the best of them, but he was always out somewhere—on the prowl, he called it. Duck was always the one to get stuck with staying at the hideout. He never stopped to wonder why this was the case and that his talking had more than a little to do with it. The boss had long since decided that he should get rid of Duck, but Laramie liked him and the man was not only good with horses but was steady in a pinch. What he might lack in secretiveness he made up for with judgment when under fire. He was one of the steadiest of them all, and such men were valuable.

"Where you from, Regan?" Duck asked and then, without pause, said, "I'm from Montana myself. Haven't been back up there for a long stretch, though. Went on the owlhoot down Wyomin' way, and started cattle rustlin' in Nebraska. Ogallala! There's a town! You ever been there?"

Cassidy grinned, remembering his last visit with Mesquite Jenkins and Red Connors and the near thing it had been when three outlaws caught him and Jenkins swimming. It had been a wild visit, but that was just what visits to Ogallala were apt to be. It was much what Abilene had been in its time, and Dodge.

"Yeah, I've been there. Came up from Texas with a trail herd."

"I made that drive twice. Fought Comanches one time. She's rough, that cow trail is, believe you me! My pappy was a Tennessee man, but we moved to Missouri when I was knee-high to a cow pony. Settled in there close to Bald Knob—you heard about those fellers?"

At Hopalong's nod he continued: "Got out of there finally and come west buffalo huntin'. I ran into Laramie first time in Tascosa, and we trailed west together, workin' a few herds, pickin' up a few horses, but always sort of thinkin' over what the James boys had been doin'—you know, trains and such? Good pickin's on those trains."

"Never tackled one," Hopalong said honestly. "Should be good pickin's here, though. You get much of a split?"

Duck Bale's face became aggrieved.

"Split? Hasn't been any split! The boss, he holds all that gold himself! She's bar gold, and it isn't so easy to get rid of it. Reckon he's figured out a way now, though."

Hopalong hesitated, wondering how many questions Duck would stand for. He finally decided he had better go about it carefully. "Reckon a man could figure a way. You sell it to somebody who knows it's crooked gold and you'll discount it thirty, forty percent."

"Know it. The boss said as much, but he's got him a play all lined up. Fact is, I figure we'll have some money right soon."

"Heard some talk about a stage job just lately. Couple of hombres killed."

"Yeah." Duck Bale did not rise to the bait. He drifted away from the subject, and there was no chance to bring him back without danger of exciting his suspicions. Hopalong sat quietly, offering occasional remarks, while Duck Bale rambled on, cheerfully pleased with the sound of his own voice and the newcomer's pleasant, interested manner.

He talked of trail herds and rustling, of tough marshals and of sheriffs. He talked of hideouts and secret trails, much of which Hopalong knew, and some things about outlaw hideouts that he did not know but which Duck assumed that he knew. Filing all this away for the future, Hopalong Cassidy waited for a chance to lead Duck back into talking of the situation in Seven Pines and the stage holdups.

Duck's obvious admiration and friendship for Laramie kept recurring, and Hopalong led him to talk of this. "Did Laramie work in that last job?" he inquired casually.

"Sure. He's the best man we got. He sure was sore when he heard about that killin'."

"Thacker? He was a gunman, and from what they say, whoever killed him gave him his chance."

"No, not Thacker."

"Lock?"

Duck looked up at Hopalong, frowning a little. Cassidy yawned and blinked. "Reckon I'm gettin' sleepy," he said, and then added, to get Duck away from his sudden doubts, "That Thacker was a tough galoot. Wonder what he was doin' down here."

"Don't know, but the boss was sure mad when he saw him! He was mad all the way through, sure enough! Said somethin' about a double-cross. Then he invited Thacker out and shot him down!"

"Takes nerve to shoot it out with a man fast as Thacker was. They say he gave Thacker his chance."

"He did, but the boss had a reason for

that, I figure. And then he's so cussed fast he don't have to worry any."

"Fast, is he?"

"Faster than Hardin, I figure. Faster than Clay Allison or any of 'em. And poison-mean when he's upset about somethin'." Duck yawned himself. "Laramie's about due," he added. "Wish he would get here. I'm nigh out of tobacco."

As Duck Bale rolled another smoke Hopalong heard Frazer stirring on the bunk. From what he had heard of Frazer, the man was surly and cantankerous, not the sort of man to accept him as readily as Duck had. While the trip into the hideout had allowed him to get the lay of the land, it had also told him something else. He now knew two of the men who had been in on the holdup. Laramie and Duck had, without doubt, been along, and it was exceedingly probable that Bud Frazer had been in it also.

No closer to the identity of the boss, he still knew some of the men, and from what he had heard, the boss was the man he wanted, the man who had killed in cold blood the wounded and unconscious Jesse Lock. Now the sooner Hopalong got away from here, the better. To come and then ride away at once would scarcely seem logical to Duck, unless . . . Hopalong frowned, trying to figure out a way.

If he could make the break without gunplay, so much the better, for he might catch the boss himself here if he was not worried about discovery.

"Better water my cayuse," he said suddenly, and getting to his feet, he strolled casually outside.

Behind him he heard a chair creak and he knew that Duck Bale was watching him. He sauntered unconcernedly across the sunlit open space to the trees. Topper nickered as he approached, and he gathered up the reins and started back toward the tank. As he turned he caught a glimpse of Duck watching him from within the door. The horse dipped his muzzle into the clear, cool water, and Hopalong sat down on a log close by. Here he was out of sight of the cabin door, and he instantly slid out from beneath his hat, left it on a post in such a way that he would still appear to be sitting where Duck had obviously seen him seat himself. Then he crawled around the corral, straightened, and tiptoed swiftly to the side of the house.

He was acting on the impression that Duck would awaken Frazer, and that he had guessed right was immediately obvious. An irritable voice growled, "What're you wakin' me up for? What's the matter with you, Duck?"

"We got us a new man."

The bunk creaked as Frazer evidently sat up, startled into wakefulness. "A what?"

"A new man. Drifted in about an hour and a half ago. Feller name of Red River Regan. Heard of him?"

"Don't recall. Where's he now?"

"Waterin' his horse. About as tall as me, but some heavier. Said the boss sent him out. He come ridin' right in like he knowed where he was. Had my name right, and yours too."

"Nothin' been said about us havin' a new man. We got enough men."

"Tell that to the boss. Anyway," Duck protested, "he's a right nice feller. Texan, I reckon."

"What's the boss want more men for? The split's too small now! Why, with Laramie, Dan, you and me and the boss, that's plenty. I don't like this feller hornin' in."

"He looks plumb salty."

"Where's my gun? I want a look at him."

Turning, Hopalong fled swiftly back around the corral, then straightened up with his hat on and led the horse across toward the trees again.

Bud Frazer stood in the doorway of the cabin, his bulk filling it. He wore a dirty shirt and patched jeans. His boots were down at the heel, and he wore a gun tied low on his leg. Unshaven and his hair rumpled, he looked tough and mean. Strolling out into the sunshine, he called out, "Hey, you!"

Hopalong ignored him, and he came a step farther. "Hey, you! Answer when I speak!"

Cassidy turned slowly, dropping Topper's reins to the ground. His blue eyes were cold as he moved coolly to one side of the horse, putting distance between them. He wanted no trouble, but he was taking nothing from anyone. If Frazer wanted trouble, he could have it. "When you speak to me right, I'll answer. Otherwise I'll answer when I please!"

Frazer sneered. "Tough guy, huh? Who sent you here?"

"The boss sent me."

"Who sent yuh? What boss?"

Cassidy felt his throat tightening. "I don't mention names. I was told not to mention names."

He seemed to have hit the right note, for Frazer hesitated. Then he said quietly, "Describe him."

"I'll describe nobody!" Hopalong replied flatly. "I don't know who you are. Far's that goes, I don't know who Duck is, except he fits the description and he isn't a man easy to mistake."

Bud Frazer hesitated. If this man had been sent here by the boss, he did not want to make trouble. On the other hand, he might be a spy. Ben Lock was reported to be in town, and having heard of Ben, Frazer had decided he did not want to be the first to meet him. This man might be Ben Lock.

"Don't you worry!" Frazer replied stiffly. "I belong here! Just see that you do!"

The big man glared after Hopalong as he turned to walk back toward his horse, and for an instant Frazer had an impulse to draw on him, but he had a hunch that warned him never to reach for a gun with this man unless he wanted to die. Fear went against the grain with Frazer and infuriated him. A naturally surly man, he feared no one and walked with a chip on his shoulder that he failed to show only around the boss. Even Laramie side-stepped Frazer. Not afraid of him, nevertheless he knew the man was easily provoked to quarrel, and needless killing had no part in Laramie's plans.

Returning to his horse, Hopalong hesitated. He was no fool and he knew that his time here was short. It was sure that some of the gang would be returning, and any one of them might have seen him around Seven Pines. Moreover, they would have come from the boss and would know no new member had been recruited. His success so far had been due to the fact that these men had not left this place and knew of none of the developments since the holdup.

Frazer watched him suspiciously, and Hopalong swore softly and wished he had managed to get away before the big man awakened. But he left the horse standing and walked slowly back toward the bunkhouse. The very fact that he was unable to get away without a fight made him irritable, and Hopalong Cassidy did not often become irritated.

Frazer stood directly in the door, and Hopalong walked right up to him before the big man gave way. Cassidy walked on beyond him and picked up the coffeepot. Rinsing it carefully, he put in some water and put it on the fire.

"Always did like a cup of coffee," Duck said tentatively. "Like to keep some on the fire most of the time."

"Same here," Hopalong agreed. "Nothin' like it."

Frazer said nothing but left the door and walked across to a chair. He spun it so the back was to the room, then straddled it, staring sullenly at the black-garbed gunfighter.

Hopalong considered his horse. The white gelding could climb back up the way they had come down, but he could not do it with a rider, and for the greater length of the slide anyone escaping by that route would be directly under fire, like a target in a shooting gallery. Nor was escape out the main trail a good plan, for there was every chance of meeting a rider coming in, and that would mean being caught in a narrow passage with no hope but to kill or be killed.

"You hombres poker players?"

"Yeah," Duck Bale replied interestedly, "I like a hand of draw now and again. Frazer plays too."

"Only"—Frazer could not let it lie—"I'm particular who I play with!"

Hopalong turned quietly and slowly. He had lifted the coffeepot and now he put it down. "Seems to me you're some on the prod, amigo. Now, I'm not. When the boss told me about this outfit, he told me it was a good crowd. He didn't say nothin' about any cantankerous vinegaroon like you. I don't think I like it as well as I did around here. If I stay, I'm sure goin' to have to kill you!"

Frazer's lips thinned. "Kill me?" he sneered. "You must figure you throw a fast gun."

"There's a way to find out," Hopalong suggested, "and you can make your try any time you've a mind to."

Frazer's fingers spread slowly, his eyes watchful as a snake's, yet deep within him there was something that chilled at the utter coldness in the eyes of Red River Regan. An utter coldness that spoke of death. A fly buzzed against the window, and outside Topper blew contentedly as he munched the thick green grass. Within the room all was still as death, and watching the black-garbed man, Frazer felt a faint, cold chill go over him.

It was here. He had been fairly called, and he knew it was up to him now. His mind told him he must draw, but no command ran along his muscles to the waiting fingers; no hammer was thumbed. Tense, he waited, his mouth dry.

And then it happened.

Duck Bale sprang the trap that Frazer had set for himself with his own quarrelsome pushing of this stranger. Duck Bale, who was harmless enough in his day, but smart too. Duck sighed.

It was a long, gusty sigh, and Bud Frazer knew what it meant. Bale had given him up; Bale had decided he would not draw, that there would be no shooting here. Through the mind of Frazer there now went a series of fleeting pictures. Of Bale crowding him, of Bale no longer avoiding trouble, of Bale repeating the account of what happened here, of how this man had taken the prodding of Bud Frazer, then called him, given him his chance. Frazer knew what they said about him. He knew he was a man avoided, if not feared. The very certainty that he would fight had built his reputation, and now this Red River Regan had called him.

There was no way out. Grim with determination, he grabbed for his gun. Yet even as he grabbed, a wild fearfulness came up in his throat, choking him with panic. His hand grasped the gun, and flame stabbed suddenly from the hand of the man before him. Frazer had stepped back off the chair as he drew, and now he fell forward, striking the corner of it and falling to the floor, the chair across him.

Hopalong glanced once at Bale, who was staring at him, his face a picture of amazement. Duck Bale had seen the best of them, and just now he had seen a gun leap to a man's hand in the fastest, smoothest draw he had ever seen! He had seen Bud Frazer, no mean hand with a gun himself, shot down with never a chance even to clear his holster!

Red River Regan was looking at him, and in those icy blue eyes there was a question. "He had his chance. He asked for it."

Bale nodded. "He—he was a trouble hunter. Always on the prod."

Cassidy saw he now had an excuse to leave and grasped it. "I think," he said, "I'd better puff out of here and see the boss. He isn't goin' to like this."

Bale nodded. "Yes. You better see him. He maybe won't mind so much as you figure. Especially as he's got you, and you're faster than Frazer."

Hopalong thumbed a shell into the empty chamber and stepped out the door. Crossing to Topper, he swung into the saddle. Bale turned back at once, and Hopalong immediately turned and went up the canyon toward the empty house and the rock slide. To be caught coming out of here was not part of his plan. At the same time he knew that the challenge was thrown now. The outlaws would have to kill him or leave the country, for he knew their hideout. Within a matter of minutes after they heard of this they would know who he was. Well, he had always crowded his luck; he would crowd it some more.

The white horse scrambled up the slide, and at the top Hopalong let him take a blow. Then he mounted and drifted.

Seven Pines was rocking and rolling. This was payday at the mines, and the boys were in to throw a wing-ding and were well into it before the weary gelding walked up to the livery stable. The saloons were crowded to the doors, and the street rang with shouts and rough singing. At least three pianos jangled along the street, and now and again the rasp of a fiddle would sound through the hoarse voices. Occasionally there was a gunshot, but nobody even looked around to see if it had been fired from pure devilry, fun, or with deadly purpose. Seven Pines, like Bodie and many another western town, was proud of its reputation for producing "a man for breakfast" every morning.

Pony Harper leaned against the end of the bar and studied the crowd with cold, watchful eyes. Tonight he would make money, but a bullet could ruin one of the tinkling new chandeliers, and he wanted to save them if he could. The chips clicked, cards riffled, and the roulette wheel rattled as it turned away fortunes on every spin.

Gray should have been here by now. It was time they got busy, and this was the best time in the world to announce a gold strike with the room full of half-drunken miners. Harper smiled coldly, contemptuously. It would serve Harrington right and kill two birds with one stone. The mine would have to shut down for lack of help, and the rush to the scene of the strike would easily cover their own find of gold.

That had been a smart idea: to start a fake gold strike, to plant a little gold around where it could be found, and then to work a vein of their own and produce a lot of gold—gold stolen from Harrington's mine!

Gold was gold, and once out of that bar, nobody could identify it. They would make their own bar, stamp it with their own name, and even if Harrington grew suspicious, which he wouldn't, there would be no way to prove anything.

A man had come in the door, a tall, cold young man with calm eyes, a young man in ragged digger's clothes, but who wore two belted guns. Pony Harper's brow creased. The man was a stranger—and then he knew!

The man was Ben Lock.

Jesse had talked a lot about Ben. Jesse had been gun-slick and everybody knew it, but the younger Lock had always bragged about how much better his brother was. After one look at this man, slim as a rapier, edged and pointed for death, Harper knew this was a man who would, having a purpose, never deviate therefrom.

Harper left his post at the end of the bar

and sauntered around, working his way through the crowd to Lock's side. The young man did not look around. "Welcome to Seven Pines, young feller!" Pony greeted him. "Stranger, aren't you?"

"No, I'm not." The voice was low and cold.

"Sorry," Harper said easily. "Didn't mean to offend you. If there's any way I can help you, just let me know."

Lock looked around, and their eyes met. Pony Harper suddenly was very glad this young man was unaware of certain things. "Where can I find Hopalong Cassidy?" Ben Lock asked.

Harper felt a leap of triumph go through him. "Cassidy?" He raised his brows. "You mean that feller who happened to show up after the stage robbery? Why, he's workin' out at the Rockin' R. Took a gunman's job."

"Is he in town tonight?"

"Perhaps. Haven't seen him." Harper was cautious. "My name is Harper. I own this place."

The young man measured him without changing expression. "My name is Lock," the young man replied. "I had a brother who lived here."

"Jesse. I knew him well. A fine feller!"

Ben Lock looked at Harper for a long minute. "He didn't say the same about you."

Pony Harper was nettled. The attitude of Ben Lock irritated him, and it offended his sense of importance. Accustomed as he was of late to being accorded some deference and re-spect, he did not like it that this cold-eyed young man drifted into town and seemed to care nothing at all about him or about what he might feel. It was something of this same atti-tude, although in a much more casual, easygo-ing sense, that had always made Harper dislike Jesse so intensely. The two young men were alike in that; they walked with a cold confi-dence in themselves, which was irritating to such a self-important man as Harper.

"That's too bad!" he exploded. "He had no reason to dislike me! And who was he to set himself up as a judge of anybody?" The con-tempt was thick in Harper's voice, but instantly the big man was sorry he had given rein to his feelings. The animosity in his voice and attitude was now obvious enough. Yet Harper was a man who had little respect for the intelligence of others, and he did not believe this young man would long remain his enemy if he han-dled the situation right.

"Oh!" He waved an airy hand. "Forget it!

I was mighty sorry about him gettin' shot like that, mighty sorry, and so were we all. Fact is" —and here he established an alibi for himself —"Harrington, the sheriff, and I were among the first on the scene. We rode up together. Met this Cassidy feller on the trail, hightailin' for town. He told us your brother was alive, but when we got there he was dead. We heard no shot from the time Cassidy joined us," he added.

"You think Cassidy killed him?" Lock demanded abruptly.

Harper's eyes grew small behind their thick lids. "I didn't say that, and I'm not goin' to say it. Hopalong showed up and we rode back and your brother was dead. Seemed funny that Cassidy should be there so quick-like after it happened. And Thacker," Harper added, "was killed by a gunfighter. He was mighty slick himself, but the man who downed him was a whole lot faster."

"I see." Lock put his glass down on the bar. "I think," he said evenly, his eyes narrow and chill, "I'll have me a talk with this Hopalong Cassidy!"

"You won't have to wait." Harper's voice was hoarse with satisfaction. "There he stands in the doorway!"

Ben Lock turned and faced the man

named as one of the most famous gunfighters on the cattle trails. The man who was, as Hickok had been, a living legend. He looked across the crowded tables, across the noisy room, to see cold, observant blue eyes, firm chin, and a bronzed, handsome face looking from under the wide brim of a black sombrero. Two tied-down guns with white handles, two guns whose use had made their wearer one of the most feared and respected men of his time.

Lock stepped back from the bar into a clear space. He looked down the bar toward the door and said distinctly, "Cassidy, I want to talk to you!"

CHAPTER 7

SHADOW OF THE NOOSE

Briefly Hopalong studied the tall young man, then nodded. "Why, sure! You want to talk right here or elsewhere?"

Ben Lock walked toward the black-garbed gunfighter, noting the steady blue eyes, watchful and dangerous, yet also recognizing at once that Cassidy was not on the prod. Ready for trouble, he would accept it but would not force it. "Most anywhere," Lock said. "They tell me you were the last man to talk to my brother."

"That's right." The knowledge of who the stranger was served to relax Hopalong, who, despite the rumors, anticipated no trouble with Lock. "He was wounded badly but alive when I left him to hunt a doctor. Somebody shot him while I was gone."

While versions of the story had been told

around town, there had been a half dozen of them and no two alike. Moreover, some of these stories had been broadcast with an aim to discredit Cassidy and make him seem a suspicious person. His clear statement to the brother of the murdered man was uttered deliberately and for its effect upon those rumors. "It isn't likely," he added, "that I'd have said he was alive if I had known he was dead. Nobody knew but what he was killed outright durin' the holdup."

This comment carried the ring of authenticity and reason. Several heads nodded, and Pony Harper saw with irritation that what he had hoped for from the meeting between Lock and Cassidy was not to be. At least not on this occasion. As the two walked to a table Pony Harper stared after them, wishing he could overhear their conversation. He was standing at his usual place at the long bar when Duck Bale came in.

Harper was the first to see him, and his brow puckered slightly. The second man to recognize the outlaw was Hopalong Cassidy, and he was instantly alert.

The outlaw walked directly to the bar and ordered a drink. Once his eyes seemed to drift down the bar, but at whom he looked Hopalong could not see, nor if any signal passed between them. If Bale was aware of Hopalong's presence he gave no indication of it. Meanwhile, Cassidy sketched briefly his actions before the holdup and for the first time told of the riders he had seen and of their tracks.

"I never mentioned that to anybody but you," he said. "And I located their hideout."

Without identifying any of the outlaws or the location of the hideout, Hopalong recounted his experiences of the past two days. Lock was impressed by the evident sincerity of the black-garbed gunfighter, and what little doubt he had was gradually lost. Whoever had killed his brother, he decided, it certainly was not this man.

Before dawn Hopalong Cassidy rolled out of a makeshift bunk in the hayloft of the Seven Pines Livery and headed out of town toward the Rocking R. Topper moved out fast in the cool morning air and Hopalong was back at the ranch in time for breakfast and to meet Shorty Montana out at the corrals. Shorty glanced around at him, grinning. "You sure weren't a-woofin' when you said there was plenty to do here! There are lots of cows in those draws east of the Antelopes."

"Keep your eyes open," Hopalong advised. "You'll be workin' that country with Tex and the Kid. Don't start trouble, but don't take any lip from anybody, either. If you see any 3 G stock, start it driftin' east."

Dusark came from the bunkhouse, walking with a swagger. His manner was belligerent. Hoppy's cold eyes surveyed him briefly, then passed on. Joe Hartley, he had noticed, was a serious fellow, and a good hand when away from Dusark. "Joe, you work with Frenchy today. Drift your stock north and make the gather at Mandalay Springs. The same for you hombres workin' the Haystack."

"What about me?" Dusark wanted to know.

"You'll be with me, Dan. We'll head over toward Rosebud."

Something flickered on the big man's face. "I been workin' with Joe," he protested. "We're doin' fine together."

"Yeah, but it's you and me today. We check the Rosebud, Rabbithole, and the edge of the desert and around by Sugarloaf."

Carp had warned him the attempt on his life would be made near Rosebud and on some sort of false message. There was a chance that Dusark himself was involved, but with the man close to him, he would be unable to slip away and alert the killers. At the same time Hopalong would be able to learn more about the big man, as well as the country, with which he was not familiar.

The sun was clearing the mountain's ridge in the east when they started out. Dusark looked surly and had nothing to say. Hopalong drifted along beside him, pointing their horses toward the narrow defile of Rosebud Canyon.

"Rustling," Hopalong said suddenly, "is over in this country. Within the month we'll have it wiped out. This bunch," he continued, "is getting too careless. Worse than those stage robbers."

"Nobody has got them yet." Dusark's voice was dry, his expression amused.

"Not yet," Hopalong agreed, "but that hideout of theirs won't be any good to 'em anymore. That means trouble, because they'll have to move and folks will see 'em."

"What hideout?" Dusark was surprised. "And why won't it be any good?"

"Why, I was there yesterday," Hopalong said casually. "Dropped in and had me a talk with a couple of the holdup men. An hombre by the name of Bud Frazer was one of them. Laramie's another, but he was off tom-cattin' around somewhere."

Dusark's surprise was evident. "You mean you found their hideout?"

Cassidy nodded. He was elaborately, deliberately casual. "It wasn't hard. Good place, though. Two men there, this Frazer and Duck Bale."

"Don't know Bale," Dusark said honestly, "but that Frazer's mean."

"He was," Hopalong agreed. "A hard man to get along with. Too bad, too. He just naturally prodded himself into a grave."

"Huh?" Dusark blinked his astonishment. "He's dead?"

"Yeah." Hopalong flicked a fly from Topper's neck. "He was a mite slower than he figured."

Dan Dusark was beside himself with curiosity. Of this he had heard nothing. He was aware that Cassidy had visited Corn Patch, for he had been the rider that Hopalong passed as he went for his horse. Dusark had heard the account of the poker game at Corn Patch from Hankins and from Harris himself. It worried him that Hopalong seemed to find his way around so easily. Despite all he had heard of the gunfighter, he had believed little of it, but now he was beginning to credit the stories.

Riding into the country a stranger, Hopalong Cassidy had almost interrupted a holdup by the fastest operating gang the country knew, and then he had whipped Hank Boucher, backed down Windy Gore, had outmaneuvered the whole Gore outfit, and then had ridden deliberately to the rustlers' stronghold at Corn Patch, beaten Harris at poker, which was unheard of, and had dared Troy to draw. He must have left there and gone right to the hideout of the stage robbers, a place not even Dusark knew. And while there he must have killed Bud Frazer.

Uneasily, Dusark considered his own position. For a year he had been spotting herds for the rustlers and sharing in the take. Did Hopalong know that? How could he know it? But how could he have known where the hideout was? How did he know a lot of things he obviously did know? And why had he chosen him, of all people, to ride to Rosebud with?

Suppose he knew of the plot against his life. Suppose Cassidy was deliberately leading Dusark into a trap of some kind. Dusark was far from a coward, but he possessed the guilty man's natural suspicion of everything he could not understand and the ignorant man's suspicion of devious methods. What Hopalong knew he could not guess; but, coupling all that had happened since his arrival with what he had heard of the gunfighter, he began to sweat.

Moreover, riding to Rosebud worried

Dusark. The trap had been awaiting only a tip-off from him. But Poker Harris was furious over the flouting of his authority and skill at Corn Patch and might proceed on his own. Somebody might have been watching the Rocking R from the hills and might have seen the two men ride toward the Rosebud. In such case the trap might be set and waiting, and Dusark had no illusions about himself. If he got killed in the process of killing Hopalong, Harris would not lose one minute's sleep over it.

Hopalong was aware of the big man's increasing worry, and he guessed at the cause of it. His own eyes were unceasingly active. The trail held no tracks, but any dry-gulchers would certainly have circled into position.

"You know," he said suddenly, "if anybody wanted to kill a man, that defile up ahead would sure be a likely spot."

Dusark started, and his face paled. He avoided Hopalong's eyes and shrugged. "Might be. But who would want to kill anybody around here?"

"I've heard tell of it," Hopalong commented dryly. "There might even be a few hombres around who would like to kill us."

"Us?" Dusark was startled anew.

"Yeah. The rustlers have got it in for the

Rockin' R, now that we've showed fight. They'd like to get rid of all its fightin' hands. That includes both of us.

"Me, naturally they'd want me. And they might figure you, knowin' the country, could tell me where the stolen cattle are taken. A few of 'em undoubtedly go to the mines around Unionville and Seven Pines, but not the bulk. They are driven out somehow. I've got a hunch they go west or north."

This was exactly right, and nobody knew it better than Dusark himself, who had assisted on some of those drives. But how had Hopalong guessed? He phrased the question, and Cassidy waved a careless hand.

"Simple. What's east of here? Wyomin' and Utah. Do they need cows? They got 'em, plenty of 'em. What's left? The western part of Oregon, California, and maybe the mines of western Montana. East they would bring small prices; west they would bring half again or twice as much."

"But how would they take 'em out?"

"Ever hear of Jesse Applegate? Or Lassen? They had a cutoff northwest of here. A few bad stretches, but from what I hear, High Rock Canyon has plenty of both grass and water. The rustlers could follow that cutoff just as easy as wagon trains did with their stock."

Dan Dusark stared at the gap before him and mopped his brow with a soiled handkerchief. If they had decided on today, the ambush would be above this defile, and he was riding into it. Moreover, what Hopalong said seemed to be true—that rustling was dead in this country. With a man riding segundo for the Rocking R who could figure as closely as this hombre, it would be too dangerous to warrant the effort. He found himself wishing he had saved his money.

His mouth was dry and he kept wetting his lips. Once he risked an uneasy glance at Cassidy, but the gunfighter rode calmly ahead. If he guessed at what might be awaiting him, he gave no evidence of it.

Several times they came upon cattle feeding and started them drifting toward the holding ground. With far too few hands for the area they had to cover, it was simpler to skirt the outer edges, gradually forcing the stock toward the point where the gather was to be made. In this way the whole problem became much simpler.

And then, at the very opening of the defile, from which point there would be no turning back if they continued, Hopalong turned abruptly riding his horse over a narrow bench into a dim trail that headed due north.

Instead of being relieved by the action, Dusark was more worried. How had Hopalong known of this trail when he himself had not known of it? Actually, Cassidy had glimpsed, from several miles back, a small patch of far-off green on the slope of a mountain to the north. That a trail must lead to such an obvious source of water he did not doubt, and presumed that a man might cut such a trail by the turnoff. That he rode into it almost at once was a surprise to him as well as to Dusark, but for different reasons.

More and more cattle appeared, and they worked hard. Dusark threw himself into the work with a will and, like many rustlers, was a good hand with cattle. Within the next two hours they started over two hundred head toward Mandalay Springs.

Meanwhile, Hopalong had been carefully searching the country for any riders or evidence of riders. Several times he left Dusark and swung wide after the few lone cattle who grazed far out from the rest, hoping to cut a trail. When he did, it was that of a hard-ridden horseman headed northwest toward the desert. Leaving Dusark to push the cattle toward the holding ground, Cassidy rode west, then struck north on the lone rider's trail.

As he rode he reflected. Most of the beef

he had seen wore the Rocking R brand. Little of the 3 G stuff had penetrated this far, and there was only a scattering of other brands. On the whole, this side of the range was fairly clean of other stock. Twice during the morning he had cut the trails of small bunches of cattle traveling northwest.

This section of the range had been worked least of all by the Rocking R riders, for the very reason that it was well grassed and relatively clean of stock from other ranches. For that reason any rustler was sure to find it a fairly safe area in which to work. It did not help that the Rocking R had been short-handed ever since the death of Old Cattle Bob.

Passing over the Rocking R grass, Hopalong rode into a cluster of low juniper-clad hills and entered them through a draw littered with rounded, water-worn boulders. The hoofs of the dun clicked and grated on the rocks as he rode, but, sighting a dim trail, he turned out of the draw and onto the hillside itself. There was sage here, and some greasewood. Bunch grass was occasionally seen, and there were patches that indicated water was not too far from the surface.

To a stranger or an eastern man this range, like that of much of the best cattle country, would have appeared dry and desolate in the extreme, and such a man would have doubted that anything larger than a jack rabbit could find sustenance along the sagebrush levels and the low, often rocky hills. Actually much of this dry, unhappy-looking vegetation was excellent stock feed, and the white-face and shorthorn, like the longhorn that preceded them, were good foragers. Looking around, Hopalong could now see indications that this range had not long since carried more cattle than it did now.

As he rode, his eyes kept drifting to the northwest, where that lone rider's trail disappeared. Out there lay the desert, and beyond it a rugged range of mountains. Somewhere over in there was High Rock Canyon with its grass and springs, and there were other water holes and a few small lakes. Not a difficult country to ride through if a man knew where the water was. But in almost any of this country a stranger might easily die of thirst within a few yards of water, for the springs or water holes were small, and in most cases they lay in folds among the rock or in hollows among the hills. Out of sight, and hopeless to find unless one acted with previous knowledge.

Everywhere he rode he saw indications that this range had been worked over within the past few weeks, and some of the cattle appeared to have been driven off within a few days. Here and there he found a few head and started them back toward the holding ground.

He was riding among some low hills, their flanks studded by flat rocks, when he saw a man ahead of him. The fellow was obviously old and driving a burro. He turned as Hopalong rode up, and sized him up carefully, then nodded.

"Howdy!" he said cheerfully. "Ain't seen nobody in a long time!"

"Where are you headin'?"

The old man bobbed his head toward the northwest. "Them rocks. Seed some mighty good float up there and come out for a grubstake. Lots of gold in this country if a body can find it."

"Been around it long?"

"Thuty year, and most of it lookin' a burro in the behind all over these hills. Know every inch of 'em."

"Must have been wild around here then. Many outlaws?"

"Sure thing. Some bad ones, too! And you durned tootin' it was wild. Right over that"— he pointed toward some low hills to the east— "I saw Cattle Bob ride down on Dakota Jack's outfit of rustlers.

"Fight? You should have seen 'em! Both

outfits were plumb salty, and Dakota Jack was sided by that poison-mean youngster, Vasco Graham! Fight started in that bottom when Cattle Bob caught up to 'em with a bunch of his cows. Rode right into 'em, and in the first blast of gunfire they shot down one outlaw and two horses. Vasco fell, and when Dakota Jack came back for him he shot Jack out of the saddle. Then he took the horse and got away."

"Dakota Jack was coming back to help him?"

"Yep. I never saw the like. The way I figure it, Vasco Graham knew that horse couldn't outrun Cattle Bob and his men if'n it was carryin' double."

"That was hard . . . mighty hard." Hopalong mused.

"Sure was, but that was Vasco. Often wonder what become of him. He knew this country like a book and was mighty fast with a gun. And mighty free with it."

"Heard somethin' about him." Hopalong frowned. "I think he shot him a sheriff over in Montana one time."

It was long after dark before Hopalong rode into the ranch yard. The Chinese cook looked up irritably as Hopalong started for the cookhouse. "Supper, he cold," he grumbled. "Why you not come on time?"

"Busy, China," Hopalong said, grinning. "Come on with the coffee. Forget the rest of it."

"Forget nothin'," the Chinese cook replied shortly. "You work, you got to eat."

The door opened, and Hopalong glanced up into the eyes of Lenny Ronson. "Oh? It's you." She seemed disappointed. "I hear you have been quite busy." Her voice was cold. "You seem to have a faculty for creating trouble."

"Some folks do," Cassidy admitted. "Personally, I don't care for it."

"Well, for a man who doesn't care for it, you seem to be in the middle all the time!" she flashed. "Now I hear you've had trouble over at Corn Patch!"

Hopalong was instantly alert. He shook his head wonderingly. "Now what trouble did I have over there? I don't recall any."

"You killed a man. You killed Bud Frazer!"

Hopalong waited for a full minute, his attention on her statement. He had told only Dan Dusark, and Dan had come in late. He doubted very much if she had talked to the big cowhand. Furthermore, that killing had taken place at the hideout with only Bale as a witness, and if he had told anybody, then he must also have revealed the hideout. Sure that he had struck a new lead, Hopalong tried to draw her out.

"You heard that? Now what do you know? Just goes to show you how folks talk about things they know nothing about!"

"I do know about it!" she protested. "You picked an argument with him and then killed him."

"Everybody in town talkin' about it, I suppose?"

"I haven't been to town. But certainly they all will be hearing about it! And they will all be saying that we hired a killer!"

"Could be." Cassidy filled his cup once more. "But I thought you wanted your brother to hire Clarry Jacks. Isn't he a killer?"

Her face flushed with anger. "He is not!" she protested. "He has shot men, but he's not a—" She hesitated, flushed and angry, yet suddenly realizing the absurdity of what she was saying. An essentially honest person, she had to admit to herself that Clarry had killed men. Moreover, some of his reasons had been very flimsy. She had accused him of it herself, and he had laughed at her. It had been a pleasant laugh, but one that seemed to express tolerance rather than respect for her.

"Anyway," she said, "even if he has, that is no excuse; I don't believe in a lot of heedless killing."

"Neither do I, Lenny," Hopalong replied quietly. "But there's no sense in the good people layin' down weapons when the others won't. Peace talk has to come from both sides.

"Your dad built him a fine ranch. He kept peace here, sometimes the hard way, but he kept it and other folks lived comfortably because of it. He didn't bother anybody except those who took the law into their own hands.

"Your brother feels like you. He's against killing, but what happens? Do other folks agree that he's right and start helpin' him? No, they rob him blind! That's what I mean by not layin' down your gun until the other feller has. Now your brother has hired me, and with luck, this place will be peaceful as a sewin' circle in about a month. The time between may be sort of roughlike in spots."

Lenny eyed him thoughtfully as he returned to his meal. Despite her irritation at her brother's hiring of Cassidy instead of Jacks, she liked this blue-eyed gunman. He inspired confidence and trust, and in him she found something of a kindred spirit too.

"You don't like Clarry, do you?" she asked suddenly.

Cassidy hesitated, knowing he was on dangerous ground. "Lenny," he said slowly, "I don't know him, but what I know of him don't appeal very much. I could be wrong. I have been plenty of times. You've brains enough of your own. You do know him, so set what you know up against what you think a man should be, and then be honest about it."

Lenny Ronson got to her feet, her face sober. "I guess I've misjudged you. I've been a fool."

He grinned at her, his blue eyes flickering with humor. "Not a bit of it," he said. "Nobody's got any corner on bein' foolish. Why, I bought a blind mule once when I was a youngster, paid all my savings for it, and you know, it was three months after I learned he was blind before I'd admit it to anybody else!"

Later, as he started out the door, he hesitated. "By the way," he asked, "did you happen to see Dan Dusark come in this afternoon?"

She turned. "Why, no," she replied thoughtfully, "I don't believe I've seen him in two days. Has he gone somewhere?"

"No, just wondered if he got back all

right." Hopalong went outside and paused on the step to roll a smoke. So Dan had not told her about the killing of Bud Frazer? Who, then, had given her that news? And who let her believe it had happened at Corn Patch?

Dusark was in his bunk, but he was awake and thinking. The day had been a busy one for him, a day full of worry. All his doubts were crowding him close tonight, and he failed to cut any one of them out of the herd long enough to dab a rope on it. They crowded in a confused snarl in his brain, and long after the others were snoring peaceably he lay awake.

How much did Hopalong know? How could he know of the secret hideout of the stage robbers? The rustlers knew of the other group, but who or what they were, none of them knew unless it was Poker Harris. Yet this calm-faced gunfighter who had been in the country but a few days did know. And how had he known of that trail today? Or of the rustlers' trail through High Rock? And had he avoided the trail through Rosebud Canyon on purpose or by accident?

He was awake when Hopalong came in, and he lay quiet in his bunk, watching the glow of the other man's cigarette in the dark. He heard the jingle of his spurs when he removed his boots, the slap of leather from his belts, and then the rustle of blankets as he crawled into bed. For a long time Dusark watched the cigarette burning, then saw it rubbed out.

Dan Dusark suddenly realized that he was afraid. It was a shocking thing to admit, but he was afraid, bitterly afraid.

He had never feared death before, except remotely in the back of his mind. Death by the gun, by stampede or maddened steer had never frightened him. He had never worried when his horse swam bad rivers. Only one kind of death frightened him, and that was death by the rope. Long ago he had seen a man hanged, and the fear had come to him then, a deep, throbbing, aching fear that was mounting these days, mounting in his throat, running in his veins.

Dusark had lived all his life in cow country. He knew the justice of the frontier. Sudden, harsh, and honest in its intentions, but unrelenting. If he was caught rustling, he would be hanged.

It was time he left the country. More than time. He would say nothing at all to anyone. He would just drift out. Let Harris rustle his own cows. The difference between the money he was making and an honest wage was not great enough to cover the fear that was eating at him. A fear that had grown, doubled, intensified with the coming of Hopalong Cassidy.

Brutal and harsh in his own way, Dan Dusark did not have it in him to hate Cassidy for what he was or what he was doing.

In the morning, Dusark decided, he would saddle up and slip away. He would head for Oregon.

CHAPTER 8

DUSARK TAKES A NEW TRAIL

Under the rules as established, the roundup organized by Bob Ronson and Hopalong was a strictly local affair. Essentially it was an effort to ascertain just how much stock was being carried, the shape it was in, and to brand all unbranded stock that belonged to the Rocking R. As much of the range was free, or partly so, neighboring ranches had been invited to send reps to check the branding.

All through the previous week stock had been drifted from the far boundaries of the ranch toward the holding ground. Shorthanded as they were, this seemed the best procedure, and the roundup itself would be handled in bunches of a few at a time.

It was hot within an hour after daylight. Dust clouds lifted slowly from the hoofs of the cattle. Among these greater clouds the thin trail of dry wood smoke from the chuck-wagon fire was lost. In the rush of work Dusark had found no chance to get away, and now he was deep in the labor around the branding fire where there would be no chance for escape until he was relieved.

Tex Milligan cut the first cow and calf from the herd and shook out a loop. The rope streaked like a bullet for the calf, and the little white-face was spilled to the ground. Milligan's pony squatted suddenly as the rope fell into place, then straightened as Tex took a turn of the rope around the horn of the saddle and dragged the bawling curly-faced calf to the fire.

Dusark and Joe Hartley were working the fire, and Dusark grabbed the calf by the ears, twisting its head around and sitting on it. Joe cast the rope loose and, grabbing the hind legs, forced one forward and one back. Held so, the calf could do nothing but bawl helplessly while Weaver, one of the small ranchers, came up with the Rocking R iron. The red-hot iron hissed in the morning air; then, as Weaver stamped the iron onto the calf, there arose an evil-smelling smoke from the burning hair. Weaver looked up toward Bob Ronson. "Tally one, Rockin' R!" he yelled. With quick cuts of the knife he put the Rocking R notches on the ear, and then the calf was freed.

Hopalong was riding Topper this morning. Frenchy Ruyters, Kid Newton, and Shorty Montana were all working with cattle, and the roundup proceeded swiftly.

At the chuck wagon John Gore watched with a dark and irritated eye. For once he was uncertain as to what course to take. Con was in no such quandary. He wanted trouble and was ready for it, but he had joined in the work with a will. A roughly energetic man, he could no more have stood on the sidelines than he could have avoided a fight. Windy was helping, too, as was Hank Boucher and several of the smaller ranchers. A few 3 G cattle had been found, and a J A Connected and a Bar L U. Dust arose in a thickening cloud, and the men's faces became gray with dust streaked with sweat.

"Bar L U, one calf!" Weaver yelled.

"Come on, you souwegians!" Hartley shouted. "Rustle some stock! We're coolin' off, waitin'!"

As a matter of fact, the roundup was clicking smoothly and fast. Hopalong, his wide black hat pulled low, was in the midst of the work, doing his and more. A calf bolted from the herd before the white gelding's outstretched nose, then dodged back and raced for a hole in the mass of cattle. The gelding spun on a dime, cut the calf out again. The white-face ducked, but Topper was ahead of it again, and the calf was forced away from the herd while the bawling cow raced wide-eyed with apprehension to see what would happen to its offspring. Hopalong's rope streaked, and the calf tumbled, then was dragged to the fire.

The heat increased with the day, and the dust cloud climbed. Frenchy came in with Kid Newton, hazing a fresh bunch of young stuff into the herd on the holding ground. Bob Ronson watched thoughtfully and sharpened his pencil before turning another page on the tally book.

The clanging of the triangle at the chuck wagon stopped Hopalong as he was shaking out a loop to go after a yearling. He drew up and slapped the dust from his hat.

"Let it go, boys!" he yelled. "Chuck!"

Kid Newton reined his bay in sharply, turning the pony on both hind feet, and raced for the wagon, riding neck-and-neck with Tex. Right behind them was Frenchy. Dusark straightened from the fire, where he had been handling irons for the last hour, and grinned, red-faced, at Hopalong.

"Gettin' her done," he said. "But wait un-

til you get into that bunch of ladinos up by
Sugarloaf."

"Bad?"

"Pear eaters. Every durned one of 'em!
Wild as deer, and they crawl around in that
brush on their knees! Fact! I seen one about a
month back, and the hair was all worn off his
knees, and his nozzle was stuck full of pear
thorns like he'd had a tangle with a porcu-
pine!"

"The old ones are smarter," Cassidy
agreed. "They get most of the prickly pear
without thorns. Used to see 'em down in Texas,
around the Bend country. They go for months
without gettin' near a water hole sometimes.
Live off the pear, which runs up to eighty percent water in good seasons."

"That's a ropin' job," John Gore agreed,
looking up from his tin cup of coffee. "You
can't herd them. You got to go in and drag
'em out one at a time. She's man-killin', that
job."

"Ever rope cows at night?" Frenchy asked.
"Now there's a creep job! I've done it down in
Texas. The wild ones, old mossy-horns from
way back in the brush, they'd come out at night
sometimes and head for the water holes. We'd
ease up on 'em and then let go a yell and
charge right into 'em!

"Out there at night nobody could see well, and any black bunch you saw might be a critter. I heard tell one time of a Mex who roped a bear. Fact."

"Don't doubt it," Dusark said. "Out in California the *vaqueros* used to rope 'em for fun. Sometimes they'd fight 'em against a big longhorn bull."

"Aw," Windy Gore interrupted, "a bull wouldn't have a chance with a grizzly!"

"That's what you say," Kid Newton objected. "One time I came on a big longhorn standin' head down in the brush, his hide all blood and dirt. One eye was gone and he'd been chewed up, but he was on his feet. I hunted around some, and just when I was about to give up I found the carcass of an old grizzly. Big one, too.

"Week or so later I was down thataway again, and that longhorn was sure on the prod. I figure he was huntin' him another grizzly."

Windy Gore stared at Newton. "That's a likely story!" he sneered. "Just the sort of a story some kid would tell a bunch of full-grown men!"

There was sudden silence, and Hopalong's eyes went to John Gore. The big rancher was head up and alert. As if by magic, the men had spread out, leaving Kid Newton facing Windy

Gore across the chuck fire. Gore was full of himself now, confident and contemptuous.

Newton was slender and quiet. His narrow-brimmed hat was battered and old. His boy's face was beardless, but his eyes were old with the ways of time and the West. Hopalong suddenly knew that Windy was a fool.

"I reckon," Newton said slowly, "that my tracks are as big as yours, Windy. And if you want to call me a liar for that story, you can start your callin'—but when you do, start reachin'."

Windy was astonished and furious. "Why, you fool!" His hand dropped for his gun butt, and Kid Newton drew left-handed and shot him through the mouth.

Windy Gore took a half step forward and fell facedown at the edge of the fire, blood all over the back of his head and neck where the bullet had emerged.

For an instant all was still. Then Con Gore stepped into the circle by the fire, his hard face brutal with passion. "You lowdown skunk. You've killed my brother!"

Newton held his drawn gun level. His voice was cool. "He asked for it," he said calmly. "He was always loose-jawed and you know it. He never would have started it unless he figured he had the edge on me. I don't hold to killin'," he added, "and I got nothin' against you Gores if you stay on your own range, but Windy run his blazer and he had hard luck. Would you be out in that circle yellin' now if it had been me who fell? I don't reckon!"

"The boy's right," Ronson said quietly. "Windy made his play and he was too slow."

"Maybe there'll be another time!" Con shouted furiously. "Maybe I won't be slow!"

"Maybe." Newton was pale but calm. "I'm not huntin' feuds nor fights. You have it your way." Calmly he holstered the gun and turned his back. At the wagon he picked up his cup and filled it with coffee. Only then did his eyes return to Con Gore and his brother. He did not look at the dead man as he lifted the cup.

Hopalong moved easily to the side of the fire. "We've work to do, and we won't get it done if we're fightin'.

"We all saw what happened. Windy was your brother and you're some wrought up. Best thing you can do is forget it."

"We'll forget nothin'!" Con blazed.

"Then remember that the Kid rides for the Rocking R!" It was Bob Ronson speaking, and his voice suddenly rang with challenge. "Remember that, Con Gore! You boys started this fuss, but the man don't live that can ride a Rocking R hand when I'm alive. If you want fight, get started now or any time!"

Hopalong felt a little thrill run through him, and he was aware of the astonishment on the faces of the others. There had been doubts as to whether young Bob would go along if it came to an all-out battle, and Hoppy was sure that the Gores had doubted it, as well as some of his own men. Now Ronson had definitely declared himself. John Gore for one was amazed and discomfited. He stared, frowning, at the young cowman.

"I realize," Ronson added more quietly, "that some false ideas have developed concerning my personal courage and my willingness to back a fight. I freely admit they came from my dislike of bloodshed and my own knowledge that I am not a leader. That last has been well taken care of. In Hopalong Cassidy I hired a fighting man who will fight if he must, but who knows also how to keep peace and when to stop fighting.

"Here and now I am serving notice that if war is started we'll fight it to the last dollar, and the last drop of blood if need be." He paused. "Let's get back to work."

Hopalong glanced at Frenchy and saw

grim approval on the rider's face. Ruyters put down his cup and moved over to Newton. He spoke clearly. "We'll ride together this afternoon, Kid."

"No ridin' for either of you," Cassidy interrupted. "You'll tend irons, Kid. Frenchy, you'll work around the fire. You'll take the places of Dusark and Hartley."

Through all the altercation John Gore had not spoken, nor did he speak now. He had glanced only once at the body of his brother. Now, when he looked across the fire at Hopalong, his eyes studied that man with a cool, detached interest. Kid Newton he seemed to ignore, as if the Kid already fitted into some category in his mind. Then he spoke loudly. "We'll finish the roundup, boys, and no trouble! Understand? No trouble!"

Abruptly he turned away. Riders drifted back to their horses or roped fresh stock from the *remuda*. Few had anything to say, but as Hopalong swung to the saddle Bob Ronson walked up to him. "Hoppy, you think John's going to lay off? Or is he figuring on something?"

"My guess would be that we are in for a war," Cassidy said quickly. "I believe he meant what he said about finishing the roundup, but I think we can expect trouble. I'm glad you've got some of the boys you have got."

Dusark closed in with him almost an hour later. The big man was hazing a half-dozen head back toward the main holding ground. "Don't trust that Gore," he volunteered suddenly. "He comes of feudin' stock. They'll never rest now until the Kid's dead, and most of the rest of us."

Hopalong glanced curiously at the big man. "You said 'us,' Dan. I take it that means you're stayin'?"

Dusark's face turned dull red. "What give you the idea I was leavin'?"

"Sort of figured it. Last night you looked mighty skittish. Glad to have you, if you figure you can stay."

Dusark drew up. His small eyes stared at Hopalong for an instant, and then he said, "I've been workin' with the rustlers."

"I knew that. Many a good man's rustled a few head in his time. It's what he does when the chips are down that counts. Take it now, Dan. This range is goin' to be split wide open. We'll have war, and unless I'm much mistaken the Rocking R will be fightin' alone."

"That's about it I reckon. All right if I stay?"

Cassidy smiled suddenly. "Why, sure! Only

if you keep on eatin' like you do, we'll have to start killin' a steer every day!"

Dusark chuckled. "I always was a big eater." He bit off a chew of tobacco. "Hoppy, Joe Hartley wasn't in this with me. He knew I was spottin' a few herds, but he took no hand in it. I just wanted you to know."

"Thanks." Hopalong turned his horse toward a draw. "See you at chow."

Dan Dusark stared after the black-clad rider and chewed slowly. His thick-fingered hand pushed back the hat on his head, and he turned once and glanced back of him. "Horse," he said quietly, "there goes a good man. I reckon you and I are holed up for some months to come."

The horse flipped his tail in acknowledgment, and Dan Dusark moved on behind his cattle. It had been a long time since he had felt loyalty to anyone or anything. It wasn't, he decided, the way for a man to be. A man needed to belong to something, to somebody or some way of thinking. What Hoppy had said was true. A lot of good men had rustled a few head of stock, but they hadn't stayed rustlers.

Remembering the cool, careful look in John Gore's eyes, he let himself think for a minute and remember that a man could die in the battle for another as well as for himself.

And from the depths of his sordid years there was wisdom in Dan Dusark. John Gore was the one to be feared. Windy was the loudmouth, Con the fighter, the strong man. John was the planner, cold, ruthless, utterly relentless—and he came of feudal stock, men who felt the ties of blood and tribe as more binding than any other.

Dusark remembered Newton, and he frowned with curious consideration. "That was a surprise," he said aloud. "I'd have made the same mistake Windy did. The Kid's got sand, and he's more than half gun-slick. More than I am. I reckon Windy knew he was dead even as he dragged steel. There was something about that spindlin' youngster that made him look mighty big right then."

Nothing stopped the work now. As if by some secret order from John, even Con Gore seemed to have forgotten the killing. They worked hard and long, and dust and profanity hung in a cloud above the hot fires. There was the smell of sweaty bodies, singed hair, and cattle hanging over the branding ground. Day by day the tallies added up in Bob Ronson's black book, and as they did, his face became more careworn and watchful.

.   .   .

John Gore rode to town on the third day. He rode only after careful thinking, and he said nothing of his plans to anyone, not even to Con. When he got to town he rode directly to the Nevada Saloon. Glancing around quickly, he saw at once that the man he sought was not in. Rawhide was. Harper's gunman lounged against the bar, watching Gore with careful eyes. Gore noted the glance, considered the man with distaste, then crossed to him.

"Seen Jacks or Leeman around?" Gore demanded.

Rawhide hesitated, his mind working swiftly. Then he nodded. "Yeah, just saw 'em both go over to Katie's. They haven't come out that I know of."

John Gore strode from the saloon and crossed the street, little puffs of dust rising from each step. Rawhide turned on his heel and walked swiftly down the room to the back office. He rapped lightly, then stepped in.

"Boss," he said excitedly, "John Gore's in town. He asked where Jacks and Dud were. I reckon this is it."

Pony Harper got up instantly, his eyes suddenly ugly with cold triumph. "Could be," he agreed. "Jacks, is it? Clarry Jacks against Hopalong Cassidy! Now won't that be somethin' to see?"

"That isn't all." Rawhide chuckled. "They'll be mighty busy fightin' each other. There's a lot of good stock on both ranges."

"All right." Harper bit off the end of his cigar. "Ride out that way, but keep out of sight until you see Dan. Tell him I want to see him."

John Gore had crossed the street to the restaurant. The place was empty but for Clarry Jacks and Dud Leeman. The two were loafing over coffee and pie. Jacks glanced up with a nod; then his casualness vanished as Gore approached him. "You afraid of Cassidy?" Gore demanded.

In the kitchen Katie suddenly froze, her flour-covered hands poised above the piecrust she was kneading.

Clarry's eyes blinked; then he laughed. "Cassidy? Now why would I be afraid of him?"

"If you aren't, you've got a job. Kid Newton killed my brother."

"Heard about it," Clarry admitted. "Didn't think the Kid had it in him. Windy," he added, "always did run off at the mouth too much."

John Gore's lips tightened. It was no more than he believed himself, but he did not like others to say it.

"I'll give you two hundred," Gore said coolly. "And a bonus for Newton, Cassidy, or Ronson."

Jacks sipped his coffee, his eyes coldly alert and pleased. "What about Dud? He's a handy man."

"Figured on him. A hundred. The bonus deal works with him, too."

Clarry nodded. "All right. We'll ride out tomorrow."

Katie worked quietly in the kitchen, but she was thinking swiftly. This meant that the rumors had been true. There would be war on the range, bloody war. In her mind's eye she reviewed the situation thoughtfully. The Rocking R would be alone, and they had few men. She needed no one to tell her where the rustlers from Corn Patch would be, and her instinct told her that Pony Harper and his influence would definitely be thrown into the balance on the side of Gore. The old bull of the herd was dead, and the wolves were closing in for the slaughter.

Remembering Hopalong Cassidy, she was not so sure they would succeed, and she was glad that Shorty Montana had joined them. Shorty would be in to visit soon and through him she would be able to send word to Hopalong about the deal between Gore and Clarry

Jacks. Suddenly she thought of something else. There was another man. A good man. A man for whom Katie had made her own plans.

As if some secret wind whispered the news across the range, the coming war became the only subject of conversation at every lonely cabin, in every crowded saloon. Men here had known the Lincoln County War, the Graham-Tewksbury feud, and other bloody battles that made western history a page of violence, victory, and challenge.

The men who profited by lawlessness were drawing together, aware suddenly that, under the hand of Hopalong Cassidy, the Rocking R might again become the power for law and order that it had once been. Poker Harris had made his own plans, and in his saloon Pony Harper was doing some careful thinking. He did not believe that Cassidy would stop what had been started, and intended to see that he didn't.

Clarry Jacks, idling about town, his smile quick to come, his eyes always cold behind their amusement, heard the news and listened. He had his own reasons for accepting the bid of John Gore when it came and his own ideas for making the most of the coming war.

John Gore arrived at Corn Patch alone. He went to Poker Harris, and they talked quietly and for a long time. When Gore left he was accompanied by three men: Drennan, Hankins, and Troy. All were heavily armed. John Gore was not a man who did things by halves. He had made his decision and intended to act quickly.

On the fourth day after the killing of Windy Gore, Ben Lock rode into town and went at once to Katie's for a meal. He did not stop to think that only a short time before he had eaten a big meal at a sheep camp. Whenever he was in town these days he found himself going again and again to Katie's.

The place was empty when he came in, and almost before he was on his stool a cup of coffee had been placed before him. He looked up from the coffee. "Katie, you're a jewel. It's a lucky man who'll get you."

It was like her that she only smiled, then grew serious. "Ben, there's a war on. Windy Gore tackled Kid Newton at the roundup and was killed. The whole country is taking sides for or against the Rocking R."

Ben Lock considered the news. Hopalong Cassidy had tried to save his brother—any final doubt he might have had was now gone. Doc Marsh would not have lied.

"Hopalong's a good man," he suggested.

"He is that," Katie said. "And Ronson is and Shorty."

"You think a lot of Shorty, don't you?"

Their eyes met briefly. "I do that. He's pure gold. I do think a lot of him."

For the first time Ben Lock knew jealousy. Montana had hung around here a good deal; he always came to Katie's when he was drunk, and she had always taken care of him. There had been some gossip, but Ben put the idea aside, although it rankled. He was on his second cup of coffee when Clarry Jacks came in.

Their eyes met and passed, but each man felt a little cold prickling run over him.

"You're Lock, aren't you?" Jacks said.

Ben turned his head and nodded.

"Heard you were huntin' your brother's killer. Luck to you."

"Thanks. I'll find him."

"It may take quite a while."

Lock shrugged. "Looks like I'm good for thirty, forty more years yet. That should be more than enough."

Jacks considered Lock anew. This man was not boasting. He was quite capable of staying with it just that long, and Clarry Jacks felt a faint touch of uneasiness. "Talked to Cassidy?" Jacks paused. "You should, you know. He was the last one to see him alive and might have been told something he's not tellin'."

"Could be."

"He told you nothing new?"

Why, he did not know, but Lock was suddenly alert. Coldly he began to consider the situation. Could Jacks himself be involved? The man was a killer—and he was without doubt a man who kept many of his actions secret.

"Not much that was new." Lock picked up a doughnut. "Looks like he'll have his hands full now."

Jacks's lip curled. "He will that. You better talk to him again—while he's alive."

"He'll be around awhile. He might," Ben added, "win this fight. Suppose he sent for the old Bar 20 outfit?"

Clarry Jacks felt a distinct shock. The point was one he had not considered. When John Gore had come to him with the offer to join him and kill Cassidy, he had been more than pleased. Sure that the Rocking R could not win, he saw a lot of his own plans maturing. The war promised the weakening of both parties. Yet he knew the stories of the far-famed Bar 20 outfit. He had heard from Carp of their coming to Snake Buttes after the wounding of Johnny Nelson, and of the fight they had made there.

"Nothin' to that Bar 20 stuff," Jacks said, rising from the table. "This fight is local and, if you ask me, my guess would be the whole thing will be finished before any help could come to him."

"Maybe, but Hopalong knows what he's about. He gets around, you know. Heard he killed an outlaw named Frazer at some hideout in the hills. Frazer was one of the men in the outfit that held up the stage when my brother was killed."

Clarry Jacks stood very still. That Frazer was dead, he knew. That Hopalong Cassidy had killed him, he also knew. But how did they know Frazer was one of the stage robbers?

He turned abruptly and crossed the street to the rooms he kept. Taking down a beautifully mounted Winchester, he said quietly, "I think it's time I played my own hand—no tellin' what Cassidy might uncover!" He went out, closing the door softly behind him.

CHAPTER 9

OPEN WARFARE

John Gore in action was a coldly efficient man. The ranch house of the Rocking R was open to attack once the riders were on the range, yet two men might make such an attack extremely costly, and it was not in his plans to make one. Irene and Lenny were at the ranch, and not even Seven Pines would countenance an attack that endangered good women.

His plan was to hit the riders while on the range, to knock them down one or two at a time with a hard-riding bunch of horsemen. With this in mind he calculated where the riders were likely to be and arranged for several bunches of fresh horses to be concealed at various points so his own horsemen could make rapid changes. His plan was to win the war in one swift, hard-riding day. That he himself was only a cog in the wheel of another man's plans, he did not guess.

Dan Dusark, riding with Hartley, saw the smoke signal that called him to Corn Patch. Knowing at once what it portended, he hesitated as to his course of action. "I'm goin' over, Joe," he said finally. "I'm not goin' to do what they want but may learn somethin' that would help Mr. Cassidy."

"Better stay away," Hartley warned him. "That Harris is a sidewinder, and you know it."

"He'll never guess I've switched sides," Dusark insisted. He scowled. "He isn't the big duck in this pond, either. I wish I knew who it was. Poker gets orders from somebody, and I figure whoever it is knows plenty about the holdups."

Joe Hartley touched his tongue to his cigarette and let his eyes sweep the range before them. "Could be," he said. "But my advice is to stay away from that sinkhole."

Corn Patch was silent when Dusark rode up the street to the saloon. The place was empty as he walked in, and he strode to the bar. Harris gave him a nod of greeting.

"Kind of quiet, isn't it?" Dusark asked. "Where's everybody?"

"Where do you think?" Poker shrugged his huge shoulders. "This here's the chance we been waitin' for, Dan. The war between the 3 G and the Rockin' R will tear this range wide open. Most of the boys have gone over to Gore, and once that Rockin' R bunch is busted, we'll sweep the range of cattle."

"Maybe the 3 G won't win."

"Huh?" Harris stared at his henchman with heavy-lidded eyes. "You crazy? Gore's got his own men, to say nothing of Clarry Jacks, Leeman, Drennan, Hankins, Troy, and a half-dozen more. They'll mop up fast, and do it in one day. We aim to finish that outfit this time, Dan—finish 'em complete. Nobody alive to make a kick or a comeback."

"Where do I fit in?"

The office door opened, and John Gore stepped into the room. Dusark felt himself stiffen slightly, knowing this had been pre-arranged.

"You spot Cassidy for us." Gore was speaking. "You bring him to us at Poker Gap."

Dusark stared at Gore. For the first time he found himself resenting their certainty of his agreement. He had stolen cattle, he had robbed a few people, but he had never led a brave man into a deathtrap. Suddenly a strange feeling came over him, a feeling that the sands had run out, that he had forked his last bronc. It was a silly feeling to have, but he could not shake off the premonition. He threw away his cigarette and rolled another. "Cassidy," he said then, "makes up his own mind. He ain't a man to be led by me or anybody."

"Try it," Harris insisted. "We'll have it all set up. All you got to do is get him into the Gap."

"Not a chance!" Dusark straightened slowly. His thick-fingered hand was on the bar. His heavy features hardened. "He isn't that foolish." His eyes turned to Harris. "Why, he outslicked you at poker, somethin' nobody ever did, and he's met up with the Gores twice and come off best each time! Believe me, he'll do the same this time. I couldn't get him into a trap if I wanted to. And I don't want to!"

Satisfaction and triumph flooded him. He saw Gore's face redden with anger, and the features of Poker Harris seemed hewn from stone. "You fools!" Dusark's voice was hoarse now. "You haven't got a chance of winnin'! You're buckin' a man now who is tougher and smarter than Old Cattle Bob ever was!"

When he finished speaking, silence hung heavy in the room. Outside, a cicada sang in the greasewood, and a bluebottle fly buzzed fretfully against the dingy window.

John Gore clamped the cigar between his teeth and looked past it to Harris. "I thought you said this man was reliable. Sounds to me like he's gone over to Cassidy."

"Does sound thataway," Harris agreed. "How about it, Dan? Where do you stand?"

Dan Dusark had taken a lot of orders in his time, from good men and bad. Suddenly he realized that, any way you looked at it, his life had been a pretty shabby, second-rate thing. He could wiggle out of this. He knew that. He could apologize for popping off, fall in with their plans, then get away and carry the news to Cassidy. Or he could face them both here and now.

If these two men were dead, the war might end. If these two men were out of it, if it did not end, certainly it would be much easier. Well, why not?

He looked up. He was a big man, almost as big as Harris, and he was unshaven and untidy, yet in that moment he felt good. He felt better than he had ever felt.

"Why, I'll take my stand with Cassidy," he said calmly, "with the Rockin' R.

"It's been a long time," he added, "since I've had a chance to ride with men like that over there, and I sort of find that I like it. I like it a lot. You always were a king-sized rat, Harris, and as for Gore here, he's a penny-ante wolf who lets coyotes do his killin' for him. I don't think either of you got a streak of decent blood in you."

He expected them to draw, and they did not. He expected anger, and none came. They sat very still for a long minute, and then Gore got to his feet. "Reckon that settles that, Poker. Let me know what you decide to do." He turned abruptly toward the office door, and for a fleeting instant Dusark thought the man would leave. His eyes followed him and then with a shock of realization, swung back to Harris. He was just in time to see both barrels of Harris's shotgun blossom with crimson, to feel the heavy thud of the double charge in his midsection, and then he was falling.

He was drawing as he fell, and he fired rapidly three times. They were not aimed shots. They could not be aimed shots. The first broke a bottle on the shelf behind Harris. The second grooved the edge of the bar, and the third caught the big man in the throat, smashed against his spinal column, and carried most of it away.

John Gore, his lips white and compressed, beads of sweat on his forehead, stared at the two men. Harris had fallen full length behind the bar, and that he was dead was instantly obvious. Dusark lay sprawled on his back on the sawdusted floor, his body a vast reddening stain.

Stepping over him, Gore went down the steps. Tough as he was, he was badly shaken now, for he had never seen two men die so suddenly or so violently. He swung into the saddle and started down the trail.

Dusark was not dead, but dying. Slowly, painfully, he dragged himself to the near end of the bar, and with a stool broke the glass on Harris's rifle rack. His hand found the Sharps .50, and he jerked it from the rack. Then he turned himself around to where he could look down the trail toward the desert. Gore was in plain sight, walking his horse.

The desert waved mysteriously over the sight as Dusark tried to steady the gun. It waved, danced, then steadied, and Dusark pulled the trigger.

The buffalo gun roared and leaped in his hands, kicking viciously against the shoulder where it had been weakly held. Three hundred yards away, John Gore felt his horse stiffen, then fall. He sprang clear and ran for the rocks.

In the saloon Dan Dusark collapsed, the rifle falling from hands he could no longer feel.

.   .   .

Back at the Rocking R, Lenny Ronson was waiting for Hopalong while he saddled his horse. Her face was pale and she looked as if she had passed a sleepless night. "Hoppy," she said suddenly, "what's going to happen?"

He looked at her seriously. "I don't rightly know, Lenny. It looks like war, but something might happen to stop it."

"The Gores won't stop now. Not unless you give the Kid to them, and they might not stop even then."

"They wouldn't and we wouldn't."

"Hoppy, why don't you hire Clarry Jacks? You could, you know. Bob would listen to you, and he's a good man."

Cassidy tightened the cinch. "Clarry already has a job, Lenny. He's workin' for John Gore."

"I don't believe it!"

"It's true. Leeman and he have both joined up and, so far as we can find out, all that outfit from Corn Patch. It's the Rockin' R against the country, Lenny."

Lenny Ronson watched Hopalong complete the saddling of his horse. Then as he mounted she caught his hand. "He's—he's actually joined them?"

"I'm afraid he has."

Her lips tightened, and she felt sick and

empty. Yet always she had expected this. She admitted it now, although she would never have admitted it before. As much as she had been attracted to Jacks, she had always been a little afraid of him. It had been her brother's attitude as much as anything that had driven her to Clarry Jacks. And he was handsome, dashing, and the best dancer around.

"Hoppy," she said, suddenly serious, "if Clarry has joined the Gores, he's no longer a friend of mine. I—I guess I've always known he wasn't trustworthy."

Hopalong waited, rolling a smoke. He had worked out answers to a lot of problems, but they lacked confirmation. He was quite sure he knew who had killed Jesse Lock. He was quite sure who had handled the robberies of gold from the mine, and that behind those robberies there were two cool-headed men with no regard for human life. He was quite sure now that he knew how they planned to dispose of the gold. Yet Lenny had known Jacks well, and he might have dropped some remark that it would pay to know.

She was hesitating, then said, "He knows this country well, Hoppy, very well. He knew it when I first met him, and he'd only just arrived in town.

"Dud said once that Clarry was a big man.

That everybody jumped when he spoke—that Corn Patch outfit, even some important men in town."

Reverting to the earlier comment, he asked, "You think he had been here before?"

Lenny's gaze turned to Frenchy, Kid Newton, and Milligan, who were loafing near the bunkhouse. Shorty Montana lay on the crest of a ridge out back, covering the approach and watching with field glasses.

"Lenny," Hopalong said, "one man, or two at most, is behind all the trouble here. Pony Harper is one of them, I'm thinkin'. Maybe Poker Harris is another, but I think he's small potatoes. That Corn Patch crowd seems to be the center for the whole show, but I think it's just a side issue. Clarry Jacks probably knows who the boss is. If you remember anything he said that would help, let me know. Clarry never worked, but he always had money, and I'd like to know who he was tied in with."

She frowned. "There was a man—a man he called Laramie. Sometimes they used to talk, always off to themselves."

Laramie!

At this moment Joe Hartley spurred his mustang down the slope. He raced around the corral and slid to a stop near Hopalong. "They're movin'!" he said. "Riders left the 3 G and met up with another bunch south of here. They headed for our line cabin at Willow Springs!"

"Where's Dan?"

Hartley looked worried. "He picked up a smoke from Corn Patch. Used to be they used that signal to call him in when they wanted to make medicine. That was hours ago."

"Any movement from Corn Patch?"

"No. But I recognized that roan of Hankins with the 3 G crowd. There's nine riders, as near as I could make out."

"All right, Joe; you stick here with Bob Ronson and China. We're headin' for the 3 G outfit an' then for Corn Patch. If anything comes up we should know, or if that bunch heads this way and the place is attacked, start a smoke on top of the ridge. We'll see that."

He led the way out of the basin with four men riding beside him. It was already past noon of a new day, and there was little time. Hopalong had no love of range war, but he knew this one had to be fought and had to be won. Actually, far to the south near Corn Patch, a decisive blow had already been struck.

Dan Dusark had died, but his death had not been wasted. Poker Harris had gone out with him, but what was infinitely more important now, he had with his last gasp fired the rifle shot that froze the 3 G outfit.

John Gore was boss. Not even the tough and hard-bitten Con ever crossed him. John was the boss, and John was gone. The swiftly attacking parties that had been due to move at once and to strike hard awaited his orders, and he had not returned from Corn Patch. That last shot had not injured him, but it had broken the back of his horse, and John was afoot in the mountains, miles from anywhere he wanted to be.

Dusark had a horse at Corn Patch, but John was not aware that Dan lay dead on the floor, the big buffalo gun beside him, and John was a cautious man. It was fully three hours after his own horse died that he finally got to Dusark's animal, but the ex-rustler's mustang was wild, and he shied away from the man who crawled toward him and felt no more trust when he got to his feet. Swearing viciously, John Gore started in a lumbering run after the fleeing horse. Holding his head high and to one side to keep the reins clear of his feet, the mustang galloped away. Sweaty, bursting with rage, and covered with dust, John Gore stopped and cursed viciously.

The carefully prepared plan of attack had awaited his return, and it kept waiting. Finally, almost at noon, Con decided to take matters into his own hands and to begin by a strike at the line cabin where two Rocking R men were expected to be. But those men had returned to the home ranch shortly after daybreak and were now riding out behind Hopalong Cassidy. Dan Dusark's bullet had wrecked the timing of the scheme, and now it was too late. The general of the 3 G outfit was panting and swearing on a sage-covered hillside near Corn Patch, while not over twenty yards away stood a wary mustang who was beginning to enjoy the game.

Led by Hopalong Cassidy, the Rocking R riders were cutting through a narrow draw, and when they emerged upon the desert, Hopalong sighted a group of tracks. Reining in, he motioned the others to halt and studied the sign carefully. Two men with a bunch of led horses. "Headin' north," he said. "Now what's the idea of that?"

"Sure them horses are led?" Milligan asked. "It might be that bunch who headed for Willow Springs."

"Those are led horses. Two riders." Hopalong spoke with the sure knowledge of years of sign reading.

They continued east and then, at Hopalong's signal, drew up again. "Another bunch. One rider." He blinked his eyes against the salty perspiration that trickled into them and pushed back his hat, staring over the sun-blasted ridges and the sagebrush flats where a lake of deepest blue covered the valley floor. That lake was a mirage, but the tracks of those horses were not. They represented something.

"Dollars to doughnuts they are stakin' out fresh horses! They figure to ride far and fast over this country, wipin' us out, and usin' fresh horses to keep up the pace!"

"Sounds like Gore," Frenchy opined.

Hopalong drew his hat down and headed east once more. The 3 G was deserted except for a corral of horses. Dropping down, Hopalong threw down the bars and, with a few whoops and waves of his arms, emptied it. Grinning, he turned to the other riders. "Frenchy, you and the Kid keep watch and warn us if anybody shows up.

"Tex, you and Shorty come with me. We'll round up all the food on this place and cache the stuff where they won't find it. All the ammunition, too. We'll set this outfit afoot so fast they won't know what hit 'em!"

Chuckling, Tex and Shorty raided the grub shelves and storerooms, carrying the canned goods and other foodstuffs out to a hole in the rocks, where they were carefully concealed. Mounting once more, Hopalong headed north.

He had a rough plan now. That first bunch of horses had been taken north, and probably toward Mandalay Springs. If they were waiting there for the riders, they could be easily found; and, once led away or scattered, it would be but a short time until the 3 G men were afoot. Riding hard in the expectation of fresh horses, they would find their own mounts in bad shape by the time they arrived at each rendezvous.

As he rode, he made a picture of the range in his mind and, by nightfall, had found two more bunches of horses and liberated them, then had driven them off into the hills.

"Smoke!" Frenchy said suddenly. "That from the home place, you reckon?"

Hopalong squinted against the sun. "No, looks as if they burned the line cabin at Willow."

"Durn the luck!" Kid Newton exploded. "I had my extra shirt in that cabin!"

"Bunk!" Milligan spat. "You never had an extra shirt!"

"What?" Newton bellowed. "I sure did! And that's more than you can say! Why, you never wore a pair of socks in your boots in your life!"

"Best way to wear 'em," Tex said cheerfully. "Cooler."

"Yeah, for a horn-heeled ladino like you!" The Kid snorted.

Hopalong chuckled as he listened. It reminded him of the old Bar 20 outfit, of Red Connors, Johnny Nelson, Lanky, and the rest.

The day was gone, limping over the horizon and trailing a few scattered flags of light behind it. The heat was already gone from the air, and coolness was coming on. In high altitudes where the air is thin, over deserts where clouds are few, the heat of day changes very swiftly to the cold of night.

As he rode he chalked up the places they had struck and the horses they had scattered. Even allowing for the fact that they might manage to catch one or two horses, the 3 G outfit would be afoot by noon of the next day. Night would revive what horses they had to some extent, but they would not be ready to take the hard riding expected of them.

Putting the places together, Hopalong could get a rough idea of what John Gore had planned. Evidently he did not know that Cassidy had recalled his riders, and expected to hit them early and fast, wiping them out two or three at a time. Evidently something had gone wrong, for they had a very late start. If his guess was correct, then from Willow Springs the outfit would have gone either north to Mandalay or south to Poker Gap. If they got to Mandalay they would find no horses awaiting them, nor were there any left at Rabbithole.

If they struck toward the south and Poker Gap, they would probably get fresh horses there, yet there was just a chance they might still be encamped at that place, waiting.

That he had guessed correctly, Hopalong did not know. Nor had he guessed that he himself was expected to put in an appearance at the Gap, guided there by Dan Dusark. That had been John Gore's plan and he had talked it over with his riders. That his failure to reappear spelled disaster, they could not know.

The 3 G riders drifted into Poker Gap on badly whipped horses shortly before sundown. Leaving their mounts in a box canyon, they built a fire and prepared supper. From a hilltop Hankins kept watch on the trail for Cassidy, and so it was that about the time Hopalong had turned toward Poker Gap, Hankins spotted a lone rider.

Hankins could not identify the man, still some distance off, and it was easy to see that by the time the rider arrived it would be completely dark. Sliding off the hill, he went back to the campfire and explained the situation to Con Gore and Clarry Jacks, who were sharing command in the absence of John. He assumed the man to be Cassidy and said as much.

"He'll bed down nigh the spring," Con said. "It isn't likely he'll move on in this dark. We'll get him then."

"Wasn't Dusark supposed to be with him?" Troy objected.

"Somethin' maybe happened to change it. Anyway, the only thing matters is he's here. Keep quiet and give him time to bed down. How far away is that spring, anyway?"

"Half mile, maybe," Boucher said. "Can't be much more than that."

"Wonder what became of them riders that was supposed to be at Willow?" Leeman wanted to know. "I don't like that. We got started late and that Cassidy is up to somethin'."

Clarry leaned back and lighted a cigarette. "Forget it, Dud. You worry too much. We're all here, aren't we? What can he do?"

"John isn't here," Boucher said. "I don't like that."

"Aw, he's probably home by now," Con said. "He'll know we're on the trail. No use to worry."

· · ·

As he spoke, John Gore was building a fire in the cookhouse stove at Corn Patch. Hot, tired, and dusty, he had staggered on blistered feet from the mountains to the town. At the saloon he found both men dead. Without touching either body, he went to the cook-house, where he began to prepare a quick meal.

Meanwhile, Ben Lock had appeared at Poker Gap on a trail of his own. Earlier that day he heard the rumor of a rich gold strike made by Clarry Jacks in a mine above Star City. He reached the same conclusion that Hopalong had reached earlier. The way to dispose of the stolen gold was to find it in another mine.

Melted down and in a new bar, it would be impossible to identify. By this means the gold could be handled through the normal channels, and apparently the rumor stemmed largely from the talking of Pony Harper. Ben Lock listened and reflected that Jacks had been loafing about town or riding with Gore, and there had been no time to hunt for gold. Nor had he, to his knowledge, been anywhere near Star City in the past week or so.

Like Hopalong, Lock had decided the crux

of the whole matter was the disposal of the gold itself. Bar gold was not so easily handled as the uninitiated might suspect, and through illegal channels it would call for at least a forty percent discount. On the surface there was no connection between Clarry Jacks and Pony Harper. They were rarely seen together and seemed to have nothing in common. Actually, Lock was convinced that they represented a strong combination and that the 3 G outfit was merely playing into their hands. John Gore was a violent, easily angered, and dogmatic man. Inclined to be contemptuous of Clarry Jacks, he failed to recognize the sharp, cunning mind behind the gunman's easy laughter and good looks.

During the night after the gunfight at Corn Patch, Jacks had ridden into town and stopped briefly at Harper's office, entering by an alley door. Ben Lock had been watching that door, and Jacks's arrival filled him with satisfaction. Starting from scratch, with no previously formed opinions of the town or its people, he had swiftly leaped to the conclusion that Pony Harper was both a politician and a crook of the first water. When Clarry Jacks left town, Ben Lock was close behind him. The trail led to Poker Gap.

Darkness found the range alive with a

sense of approaching strife. John Gore was finishing his meal in the cookhouse at Corn Patch. Ben Lock made camp at Poker Gap Spring, and the 3 G lookouts who saw him arrive leaped to the conclusion that he was Hopalong Cassidy. Hoppy himself, with four Rocking R riders, approached from the northwest. And while the 3 G riders waited, Clarry Jacks slipped away in the darkness after a muttered word to Dud and rode away toward the southeast.

Clarry Jacks had the instinct of an animal for changes in the weather, only his instinct was for changes in the attitude of a locality. He was a man who knew when a game was played out, and he was shrewd enough to see that, whether Hopalong was killed or not, this country was going to be unhealthy for a long time to come.

He was a man utterly without loyalty or scruple. Dud Leeman he accepted because of his usefulness and sheer brutal courage. Jacks wanted one thing now. At first he had wanted the Rocking R, too. Now he wanted only the gold, and he wanted it alone. It was natural that he thought less of Cassidy at that moment than of Pony Harper.

Halting once, he glanced back over his trail, his cold eyes watching the horizon he had purposely crossed. No stars were blotted out by any following rider. He turned then and continued on his way. It no longer concerned him that Gore was making an attempt to waylay Cassidy. He hoped they would be successful, but to his cold, utterly egotistical nature the result was of little importance to him. The plan to dispose of the gold would have to be junked now. He would go to the hideout, remove whatever was of value there, and then go on to the mine at Star City and pick up the gold.

Returning, he would visit Corn Patch and remove Harris, then go to town again to get Pony Harper. He wanted no vengeful enemies left behind.

Later, if the war was successful and left the Gores in control, he might drift back into the country, but he had no idea that he wanted to take the chances offered by indiscriminate killing.

Riding fresh horses borrowed from the *remudas* left by the 3 G, Hopalong Cassidy led his men into a rocky defile. Overhead the stars were bright in the narrow alley of sky they could see. Before and behind was darkness, and there was no sound but the click of hoofs on rock, the creak of saddle leather, and the occasional blowing of a horse.

Long experienced in range-land warfare, Hopalong was too shrewd to ride straight into Poker Gap. He was circling through Rocky Canyon, planning to cross a saddle into the Gap so any watchers at the openings would be unlikely to see them. An hour later he made his own camp.

Frenchy scouted ahead, then returned. He was worried. "Hoppy, there's two camps. We can look right down on 'em. The one in the Gap is right out in the middle by the spring. It's a fair-sized fire but that same hombre has another fire hid in the rocks, back maybe thirty feet from it."

They crawled up to the edge of the steep slope and looked down. It was as Frenchy had said. Hopalong stared, then nodded. "Plain as print, Frenchy. Look at the reflection from that small fire. Reflects off rocks around it. I'll bet nobody could see that fire unless they were above it like we are. That hombre has built him a regular campfire for folks to see, but he don't want himself spotlighted over any fire. He's got him a concealed fire back in the rocks where he can cook a meal without bein' seen. Same time, he can watch the bigger fire."

"Well, I'll be hanged!" Ruyters nodded. "Sure as rain, that's it. Wonder who he is?"

"Let's have a look at the other fire."

This was a small fire, by which they could see the shadows of a number of men. "There they are, sure as shootin'!" Milligan whispered. "There's nine, ten men down there!"

Hopalong studied the situation. They could all see that these men had chosen a position carefully concealed, and it was probable that lone camper by the spring did not know of their existence, nor they of his, although the last was less probable. To start a fight in this darkness would mean danger for friends as well as enemies, and he had no intention of forcing a battle now if he could help it.

Sliding back off the ridge, he hunkered down behind a boulder out of sight and rolled a smoke. "Now down there is a passel of trouble," he said, "and the question is, how to handle it without too many of us gettin' shot up."

Shorty Montana snorted. "Just ride in on 'em, shootin' with both hands. They'd be so plumb surprised they'd never get a shot off."

"Maybe," Hopalong admitted, "but I've got another idea. Isn't much as ideas come, but perhaps she'll do."

Quietly he explained, and as he explained, the men began to chuckle. Battle-loving as the four were, and ready enough to run every last doubter of the Rocking R out of the country, they also had a rough sense of humor and the

zest for practical jokes no cowhand ever out-
grows. That the joke, if such it could be called,
would be coupled with disaster to the enemy
was all the better.

"First off," Hopalong asked, "who's the
best Indian in the crowd? Two of 'em, in fact."

"Me," Newton said promptly. "I was
raised up with Utes. I could steal the hide off a
longhorn calf without the cow even knowin' I
was near."

"Aw!" Tex interrupted. "Don't you believe
him, Hoppy. He couldn't find a barn in the
daytime even if he had a rope tied to it. Besides, he's too young. He's just outgrown his
rattle!"

"Huh!" Kid Newton grunted. "Leastways I
outgrew mine. Yours is in your head!"

"All right, you can both go. I want you to
slip down and get those fresh horses out of
there. Don't bother with the beat-up ones. You
can tell 'em easy enough because if they aren't
still wet, the hair on 'em will be dried an' stiff."

"And don't get your head kicked off,"
Shorty advised, flattening his shoulders back
against a boulder. "Although why either of you
needs a head beats me."

Muttering their replies, the two slipped
off. Frenchy Ruyters rolled over and nodded
after them. "Fact is, the Kid's pretty slick," he

said. "Tex, he does all right, but he cain't hold a candle to that Kid."

He watched Hopalong getting to his feet. "Where are you aimin' to go, Hoppy?"

"Scoutin'. I figure I'd like to know who that hombre is down there by himself. You two stick here and get set to cover those boys if they need it. When I come back we'll take up the rest of the action."

The steep hillside before Cassidy was covered with gravel dotted with bunch grass and occasional greasewood. A few scattered juniper added to the growth and offered some vague shelter as he started down. Nevertheless, because of the danger of sound caused by rattling gravel, it was a painstaking task to work one's way across that steep slope in darkness.

Already the second of the two fires was almost out, but the former had been replenished in the last few minutes. Only a few coals shone where the stranger had camped. Hopalong Cassidy circled around and came up on the fires warily. He was within a dozen yards of them when he heard a soft whisper of sound. Tensely he waited, listening. Then he heard it again! The sound of rough clothing moving through grass or brush! Someone else was crawling not a dozen feet away, and in the same direction! Still listening, Hopalong heard another movement on his left and realized that several men were crawling alongside him, all of them bound for the campfire up ahead. But had they seen the smaller fire? He doubted it, doubted that it could be seen from anywhere but overhead. Hopalong edged himself nearer the crawling man, caught his head outlined momentarily against the starlit sky, and slammed down with his six-shooter. With a grunt the man subsided where he lay.

Silence.

Suddenly a wild yell rent the night, and on the signal the men arose and charged the fire. They charged, then slid to a stop, looking foolishly about. Where the sleeping man had seemed to be lying was only a double row of stones covered with a blanket.

"Gone!" Hankins swore. "That durned Cassidy's outsmarted us!"

Hopalong grinned in the darkness. Straining his eyes and shifting his head from right to left because of the boulders, he soon saw and was able to identify several of the men: Con Gore, Dud Leeman, Drennan, Hankins, Rawhide!

"Hey! Where's Troy?" Hankins yelled. "What happened to him?"

"He was with us a while back. What's he doin'? Hidin' out?"

Hopalong slid hastily back into the darkness and moved for the slope. He still did not know who the stranger was, but the man must have been close by. There had been no chance for him to have escaped without being seen or heard by Hopalong himself.

A startled yell warned him that Troy had been found. And he could see the darker blotch where the men had gathered. Then he moved on up the hill and returned to his own men. He was surprised to find Kid Newton and Tex Milligan arriving, too. Both were stifling laughter.

"Got all their horses!" Tex whispered. "They are sure enough afoot now."

"You know," Hopalong said suddenly, "I didn't see Jacks, but his sidekick Leeman was there."

"Then it must have been Jacks!" Newton leaned forward. "We found one horse missin'. His picket rope had been left lyin' on the ground, but he was gone. I felt in the ground for tracks and found where a man in fairly new high-heeled boots had mounted that horse!"

"Where would he be goin'?" Ruyters asked.

Hopalong knew that Kid Newton was thinking the same thing he was: that Clarry might have gone to meet Lenny Ronson. Then another thought came to him. Suppose he had gone to the hideout? It was not too far from here, and if he knew of it he might go there. Perhaps he was the leader!

The man who had killed Thacker had been a fast hand with a gun, and Clarry was that. Instantly, Hoppy knew what he had to do.

"We've set 'em afoot, boys," Hopalong said suddenly, "and it's a good thirty miles to the 3 G. Unless they gamble and take a roundabout route, they won't get there until tomorrow night sometime. You might's well head for home."

"What about you?" Ruyters asked.

"Why, I've got a little job to do," Cassidy said, "down the trail a ways. You boys head for home. I'll be along tomorrow or the next day." He yawned. "Come to think of it, we all need sleep. Daybreak will be soon enough to move."

But at daybreak they did not move, for they were scarcely on their feet when they heard a wild yell from the valley and then a storm of curses. Saddling up, Hopalong grinned at Frenchy. "Now what do you suppose those rannies are so all-fired upset about?"

Kid Newton was grinning as he slouched toward them. He wore his left-hand gun with the butt back, but the right-hand one with the butt to the fore. Both guns ready for a left-hand draw. "Might as well have some coffee, Hoppy," he said. "I sort of figure on stickin' around long enough to see those hombres on the hike."

"Don't get too close," Milligan warned, "or they'll have that bronc of yours and you'll be walkin'! They've still got guns."

Shorty Montana had walked to the edge of the bin and was standing in plain sight, looking down upon them. "Hey!" he bellowed suddenly. "Hey, you fellers!"

As one man, they wheeled and stared upward at him. "Get movin'!" he yelled. "It's not more than thirty miles or so! If you're lucky, you make it tonight. That is—if your feet hold out!"

Con Gore swore viciously and grabbed his rifle. Instantly Shorty dropped to his knees, then rolled back away from the rim of the canyon. When he got up he was laughing, but he was careful to avoid the edge of the hill, where he could be skylined.

Saddling up, Hopalong Cassidy started east once more, but now he was riding with a definite purpose, for ahead of him was a gunman the equal, if not the superior, of any he had ever faced.

Before him the tracks lined out, easily identified as those of the horse who had been picketed where Newton indicated the man had mounted. There was a chance he was mistaken, but all the signs pointed this way, and Hopalong Cassidy was sure he knew where the outlaw was riding.

And then into the trail came another set of tracks. These were those of an unshod horse, but the rider was no Indian.

Who was he then? The mysterious camper in the canyon?

Another rider on a gun trail?

A friend or an enemy?

CHAPTER 10

A SHOOT-OUT

Recent events had Pony Harper worried. By now there should have been news. However, the few riders who drifted into town reported they had seen neither movement nor shadow on the range of either the 3 G or Rocking R.

It was uncanny and unreasonable. Knowing the rough-and-ready violence of range war, he found this silence nerve-shattering. By rights plenty of trouble should have been popping, and while one cowhand did admit to hearing gunfire, he had seen nothing. A Harper scout, riding around by the 3 G, found a deathlike silence, empty corrals, and no visible life.

Having depended upon this range war to rid him of his rivals, Harper was now thinking less of the Ronsons than of one or two others. Ever since Thacker had been found dead and his pockets empty of all papers and money, Harper had been worried. If Thacker had carried anything incriminating, that evidence might now be in the hands of his killer— and Pony Harper knew exactly who that killer was.

Four hands, he finally learned, had returned to the Rocking R, but Hopalong Cassidy was absent on some mission of his own. What if he had gone again to the hideout? What might he uncover there? Or at the mine near Star City?

Harper had a feeling that fate was closing in around him. He ran a finger around his collar and swore bitterly. Just when everything was going right! Of course if anything happened to the Gore outfit, Clarry Jacks was riding with them and the gunman might be killed. That possibility pleased him, but a lurking doubt remained, for Jacks had shown an unerring instinct for staying alive. There had been that other time, when Dakota Jack's gang was wiped out. Uncomfortably, Harper recalled what had happened to Dakota Jack. Clarry was definitely dangerous.

Joe Turner crossed to him at the bar. Turner jerked a thumb at Harrington, who stood nearby. "He was askin' for you."

Harrington was smiling when Harper stopped beside him. Harper mopped his face. "Hot," he said.

"Uh-huh." Harrington was cheerful. "And getting hotter. They found Poker Harris and Dan Dusark, both dead, and they said it looked like a shoot-out."

"I figured they worked together."

"Maybe. Can't tell where a man stands these days."

"Anybody else around Corn Patch?"

"Deserted."

"If John Gore's dead," Harper suggested thoughtfully, "that fight may be over."

If Gore was dead, the fight would be over. Harper mopped his face again. Then Cassidy might help Lock in uncovering the killer of Jesse, and that the two might fail, he doubted. His mouth felt dry and he scowled, glaring at his reflection in the bar mirror. That trail might uncover a lot of things, and suddenly he felt tired and afraid. All his plans would go for nothing—nothing!

Another worry was the gold. It had been taken to the mine at Star City. Rawhide was not available to watch over it, for Harper had foolishly allowed him to join the 3 G with Jacks. Rawhide could keep an eye on him there but had no excuse to follow when the big gun-fighter went off on his own. Always before he had been positive that he could control Clarry Jacks, yet uneasily he began to recall that such had never been the case. Jacks had gone his own way, always listening to Pony with apparent respect but then doing much as he pleased.

Harris dead. The king of Corn Patch had seemed invulnerable. Somehow he had been a symbol, for not even the domination of Cattle Bob had been able to shake his control of that corner of the mountains. Weakened, yes. His area of control narrowed, but nevertheless exis-tent. And now Harris, who had seemed as im-mune as the mountains themselves, was gone, puffed out like smoke. Pony Harper licked his dry lips.

He had slept little and looked it. His nerves were fine-drawn and he was irritable. He walked to the door and stared up the street toward the livery stable, where the arrivals stopped first.

"Wish we'd hear somethin'!" he said an-grily. "This silence gets on my nerves!"

Harrington looked at him thoughtfully.

"What stake have you got in this? You aren't with the Gores, and the only other bunch that suffers will be the rustlers. Unless," he added carefully, "unless it's the stage robbers."

"You implyin' I had anything to do with them?"

"You?" he asked innocently. "Who would think a thing like that?" He paused. "Jacks? Now that's another story. He always did have money, but where he got it I could never guess." He lighted a cigar. "See you around, Pony."

Harper stared after him, his lips compressed. He must watch himself.

Joe Turner watched him and smiled secretly. If Harper was out of the picture, Turner stood to gain more than he would lose. Ever since Hopalong Cassidy arrived, Turner had been glad he was a small man, a man unnoticed and usually out of sight. He liked it that way. It was better to be a small man and a live one.

John Gore finally caught a horse. Not the one he had chased earlier, but another horse freed from somewhere and wandering to the only home he had known. Mounted once more, Gore raced for the 3 G, arriving to find empty corrals and silence. There was neither food nor ammunition, nor any sign of his brother or the men. Wild with worry, he ran to the crest of a nearby hill and searched the desert with his field glasses. At first he saw nothing, and then only a thin dark line that seemed to move.

Squinting, he could not make out what or who it was. It might be cattle heading for a water hole. Actually, it was his own men, lips cracked from heat and thirst, dust-covered and evil-tempered. A half-dozen killers, bitter, vengeful, and hair-triggered of temper. Most vicious now, if not the toughest, was Troy, his normally vile temper aggravated by the blow from Hopalong's gun.

John Gore did some fast thinking. Most of all he needed a horse, but there were none on the ranch now, Cassidy having driven them far out onto the range. Nor would there be any at Willow Springs. The closest horses he knew of were at Mandalay. Unknown to him, these, too, had been driven off.

He returned to the battered mustang he had ridden to the ranch and swung into the saddle. The little horse started off gamely, and then Gore's mind suddenly leaped to the Rocking R.

It was nearer than Mandalay Springs. Their riders should be all gone; there should be plenty of horses. He made a decision and al-

tered his course due west. In such little deci-
sions are the courses of men laid out. For John
Gore had taken the trail to death.

Had he gone to Mandalay he would have
arrived on a spent horse, with no fresh animal
to be had and nothing to do but wait until the
horse recovered or somebody came along. He
would have been safely out of the fight until it
was over. Taking the road to what he believed
would be an almost deserted ranch, he took the
road to a ranch where everybody was home but
two men. Hopalong Cassidy was riding to the
outlaw hideout, and Shorty Montana had
slipped away from the others and was trailing
Hopalong, wanting to be on hand if he needed
assistance, and knowing that where Hopalong
was, trouble would be.

Under the flat hot sun Hopalong drifted
due east, then swung south. South of him
loomed the sprawling foothills and first peaks
of the Trinity range, and from under the brim
of his wide hat his hard blue eyes searched the
sweep of desert before him, starting near and
then reaching out, sweeping the sagebrush
levels with a careful, searching gaze that left no
hummock, no boulder, no suggestion of move-

ment unseen or unstudied. Sweat trickled down his neck. Fine white dust lifted with each footstep of his horse and settled in a film over Topper's sleek white coat and over Hopalong.

Greasewood mingled with the sagebrush and occasional patches of prickly pear, or even cat's-claw. He saw the curious twin tracks of a walking antelope, the hindfoot placed precisely back of the forefoot. Running, the track would be different. The tracks were narrower and tapered more than those of a deer.

Considering the matter, he was quite sure that Duck Bale did not know that he had come down the slide into the hideout, and it was very likely it had never been attempted by any of them. If such was the case, he might again get into the canyon without attracting attention. He mopped the sweat from his face and stared into the heat waves. The broken ridges that were the only outward indication of the hideout showed before him, and he skirted them, seeking the juniper tangle where he had found the sloping ground that led him to the slide.

The heat was oppressive, and several times he glanced at the sky, for it reminded him of nothing so much as the Kansas heat that precedes a bad thunderstorm. There was a faint suggestion of grayness over the mountain, but it might be his imagination and nothing more. In any event, his slicker was behind his saddle. He had not worn it since the day of the holdup.

For the first time he remembered the papers taken from the pockets of Thacker.

In the rush of events that followed his discovery of Jesse Lock, he had forgotten about those papers, forgotten them completely!

Pushing steadily on, Hopalong sighted one of the granitic upthrusts that marked the earthquake fault and, riding toward it, saw the junipers above him. Circling and weaving among the boulders, he arrived and swung to the ground above the slide. Taking down his slicker, he thrust his hands into the capacious pockets.

The forgotten wallet was there, several letters, and some money. The first of the letters was addressed to Sim Thacker, Mobeetie, Texas.

Inclosing one hundred dollars. On arrival you will receive four hundred more. The balance of the fifteen hundred dollars will be paid over when the job is completed. Of Clarry Jacks you may have heard. How, where, and when is up to you, but the sooner the better.

H.

That H. could stand for Pony Harper. Obviously he had sent out for a gunman to kill Clarry Jacks. If, as Cassidy believed, Harper was involved in the holdups with Jacks, then he had either decided it was foolish to share the proceeds or had decided Clarry Jacks was too dangerous to have around. The killing of Thacker now made sense. He had been called aside, given his chance, and killed as a demonstration of the futility of hiring anyone to kill Jacks. It also implied then that Jacks knew who had hired Thacker.

Why, then, had he not acted against Harper? There could be only one reason. Because he was using him and wanted him around a bit longer. The next letter was a further explanation.

In answer to your query regarding Clarry Jacks. The name is unfamiliar, but the description tallies with that of Vasco Graham, of the Bald Knob family. If this is the same man, he is wanted here for killing a man some fifteen years ago. I believe that he was involved in a cattle war in the state of Texas and he later worked with Panhandle rustlers. He is known as an out-and-out killer, and fast with a gun. He is also wanted for robberies in Colorado.

There was a circular listing rewards for the capture of Vasco Graham or his killing, and a commission as deputy sheriff. Evidently Sim Thacker had gone to great lengths to give his projected killing the cloak of legality.

There was a letter from Thacker's wife, from whom he was separated, and into this letter Hopalong put what money there was to forward to her when he again reached a post office.

Vasco Graham was the outlaw who had murdered his partner and leader, Dakota Jack, and stolen his horse for a getaway. It had been a cold-blooded murder as bad as that of Jesse Lock. No wonder Clarry Jacks had known the country!

Picketing Topper among the junipers, Hopalong went to the slide and studied it with care. There was nobody in sight, and careful inspection showed only a thin trail of smoke from the cabin where he had talked with Duck Bale. Going down the slide was a problem, not so much the difficulty as the necessity for quiet. Loose rocks made it virtually impossible, but by keeping to the inner wall it might be done. Checking his guns for the last time, Hopalong hitched up his belt and started down.

Six miles behind him Shorty Montana was working out Hopalong's trail through the sagebrush. Ordinarily, as Hopalong had taken no trouble to conceal it, this would not have been difficult, but dust devils had skittered across the desert and wiped out the trail here and there. Montana continued to move and searched the range ahead of him for some sign of Hopalong's objective.

Mopping his tough brown face, Shorty cursed the heat. He wished it would rain. He would give anything for rain. He rolled a smoke with damp fingers and lit up. Drawing deep, he stared at the wreck of mountains before him. Something, he reflected, had raised hob here. Overhead a buzzard wheeled in lazy ellipses, swinging wide and calmly. The buzzard was in no hurry. In his experience everything eventually came to him.

Shorty spoke to the horse, and it moved on, pleased to be going anywhere that might offer relief from the sun. The range over Seven

Pines was topped with cloud. He might get his wish. It might rain.

The stone house in the amphitheater had been built by some vanished tribe of Indians, and it was snug and cool, shaded from the sun. A bottle was open on the table and Clarry Jacks sat bareheaded before it. Damp brown hair was plastered against his forehead, and he was smiling at Laramie.

"You talk to Duck?" Laramie asked.

"Not me. He's a nice hombre, but let him get started and he'll jaw your arm off."

"You think that Red River Regan was Cassidy?"

"Sure. But how he found this place I'll never know. Every time I go out I have trouble getting back."

"You think he'll come here again?"

"Sure. And when he comes, we'll bury him. Duck's watchin' the entrance, and he's to let him ride right in." Jacks looked up, measuring Laramie with his cold eyes "This here's the showdown. Harper hired Thacker to kill me. He tried to hire Jesse Lock."

"Jesse wouldn't hire out to kill anybody."

"Pony tried him. I saw 'em talkin' and

braced Jesse about it afterward. He wouldn't give me any definite answer, but he did ask if we didn't get along, Harper and I."

"That was enough?"

"Sure it was. Harper wants all that gold. Every bit of it."

Laramie shrugged. "I never did trust him."

"Well, in a short time we'll be through with Cassidy. Then I'll settle with Harper. He might have tipped us off to something else that was good if this thing hadn't busted wide open. We'll slope out of here, cash our gold in for money, and live high and handsome for a while."

"Wonder what happened to John Gore?"

"No tellin'. His horse was dead at Corn Patch. Harris and Dusark dead in a gun duel." Jacks shrugged. "Didn't think Dusark had it in him."

"No." Laramie shifted his seat. He stared disconsolately at the bare table and the bottle. Was this all it came to? Hiding, dodging, waiting to trap a good man and shoot him down? "Makes an hombre think," he said suddenly. "Poker Harris was tough. I'd of said he was one of the ring-tailed terrors, and blam! He's out like a candle! If he can get it so easy, anybody can."

They sat silently, and in the distance thunder rumbled. Both men looked up. "Rain! Man, we can sure use it! Cool things off."

"Lucky, you knowin' about this place," Laramie said. "A man couldn't find it in a year, just lookin' without knowin'."

"Dakota Jack found it. He was ridin' ahead of a posse and ran up this draw. Back there where the stone gate is, there was a lot less opening than now. He dodged in there and the posse lost him. He found the spring and holed up here for a week, eatin' what grub he had left, a few rabbits, and some prickly pear. There was some maize growin' wild here then, too, he said.

"We used it from time to time in the next year or so, but after the outfit got shot up there was nobody left but me who knew where it was. I packed in a stock of grub and began usin' it for a hideout when I was on my lonesome."

"Wonder what caused it? That sure isn't washed out by any stream! Those jagged edges look like the ends of a broken bone."

"Man in El Paso told me it was an earthquake fault. He said the line of fault might run for miles."

"What happens durin' a quake?"

"She grinds around some. I've never been here when there was one and I don't think anybody ever was, but there's been cracks in the floors, and once a whole wall was shaken down."

The two men smoked in silence, and then Clarry walked back to the fire, stirred it a trifle, added wood, and began to make coffee.

"What's the deal on Cassidy? We let him come in, you say?" Laramie asked.

"Sure. And we take him from the front, and Bale from behind. He'll be caught in the open and he won't have a chance."

Hopalong Cassidy was already in the canyon while Duck Bale still watched outside. The afternoon was well along, and the clouds were piling up higher and higher above Seven Pines. In the bottom of the canyon Hopalong neither realized this nor cared. He was intent upon one thing only, to get within shooting distance of the man or men who had been responsible for the murder of Jesse Lock. Whatever else they had done was beside the case in his consideration. To shoot a man already sorely wounded and helpless put the killers beyond the pale.

Close to the wall, partly concealed by an angle of rock, he considered the situation. Smoke was rising now from the house in the amphitheater, and that told him that there were men not only in the outer canyon where his fight with Frazer had taken place but also here in this reconstructed Indian house among the evergreens.

There was cover in plenty here, and he used it, moving carefully around by the rocks and working his way closer and closer to the house. The two men within were men worthy of his guns in every sense. Either might prove his equal; together they might be far superior. In any event, it did not pay to take chances with such men. One mistake was all anyone could expect—and that one would be fatal.

Thunder rumbled again, nearer this time, and Hopalong paused, noting it and carefully considering what it might mean to him. Then he moved on.

A half mile away, at the mouth of the fault, Duck Bale arose and stared off toward Seven Pines. All was blackness over there, a blackness shot through with vivid streaks of lightning. The front of the storm was rolling down upon him, and he did not like his situation one bit. Any fool could see that he was going to get wet if he stayed where he was, and maybe struck by lightning on that high, exposed knob of stone. He turned, and glancing back toward the canyon, he felt himself start. Someone was creeping along the far wall of the amphitheater!

Instantly realization came to him. Hopalong Cassidy was already inside the canyon!

No sooner had he realized this than he began to scramble down the rock, just a minute too soon to see a rider turn in the mouth of the draw and stare his way. That rider was Shorty Montana. He had finally lost Hopalong's trail and was hunting for it in that maze of uptilted rock.

Bale hit bottom and broke in a run for the shack in which Laramie waited. Now they had Cassidy! Had him bottled up!

But how had he gotten in here? There was only one alternative, and that was the rock-slide, but Bale had examined it, and it had not looked too practical, as a man was sure to make noise descending it. He hurried to the door of the stone building and shoved it open. Laramie was sprawled on a cot, reading a magazine.

"Cassidy's inside!" Bale gasped out. "How he got in I don't know, but he's in! I saw him!"

Laramie got to his feet and belted on his guns. His heart pounded and his mouth was dry. He knew what he was going up against, and despite the odds, he was not comforted.

Hopalong had reached the back of the hollow and was now near the corrals. The paint horse he had seen in the holdup was still there, and with it now were six other horses. There were no saddled horses in sight. If Clarry Jacks had intended to return to the outfit at Poker Gap, he had changed his mind or left his horse in the outer corral.

The stone building was rectangular and two-storied, although the upper story had not been entirely repaired. Its back was close to the wall of the cliff itself, and the corrals were a short distance away.

Scattered pines and firs completed the picture, and several of these were close around the house, three or four between it and the corral. The cliff wall, a part of the fault, was of sandstone, and projecting layers of it formed a partial roof over the house itself. Sliding carefully around the corral, Hopalong worked his way through the debris that lay between it and the wall. Here there were several niches, which his mind noted and filed away for future reference.

The easiest way into the building appeared

to be through a ruined corner on the second floor, but it left open the possibility that they would hear his footsteps below. Yet if this house was like many others, the intervening floor would be of stone, and he might be able to cross it without noise to warn those below.

Clouds were rolling over the canyon now, and someone inside struck a light. He was about to move forward to the wall of the house when he saw the ears of the horses go up sharply. All of them were looking inquisitively toward the entrance, and Hopalong crouched quickly, his right hand on his gun, waiting.

Movement showed suddenly, then vanished, and he knew someone from the outer canyon had slipped in. Someone who moved warily. He had no friends around of whom he knew, unless Ben Lock had found this place, which was improbable. The only alternative was an enemy, and one who knew he was here.

The man before him was Duck Bale, gun in hand, coming around the wall, still some distance away but on Hopalong's very trail.

Crouched at the corner of the corral, Hopalong considered his position anew. There was a chance he might be able to shoot his way out of the corner he was in and get away safely, yet it was not his nature to turn from a course once planned. At the same time, he did not wish to commit suicide. Long experienced in affairs of the gun, he knew full well that the best way is often straight ahead, and that was the course he chose now. He had planned to face the killer of Jesse Lock, and the man was inside this house. He was going in after him; then he would face things as they came.

Leaving the corral in a quick dive, he reached the corner of the stone house. The space here between the house wall and the sandstone of the canyon was narrow, and the light was not in the back of the house. Pausing only an instant, he gathered himself, then jumped straight up and caught the roof edge in his fingers. He chinned himself, got an arm over the parapet, and then a leg. A moment later he lay flat on his back on the roof.

Laramie had not seen this movement. Neither had Bale. Both men were looking around the corral. Behind Laramie a boot crunched and he whirled, gun in hand. Already it was nearly dark and he could just make out the face of Bale.

"So where'd he go?"

"Durned if I know! I sure saw him here, honest! Where could he go?"

. . .

Hopalong had already answered that question by two quick steps into the upper room of the house. Here he paused, listening. Outside he could hear whispers of more than one man.

Feeling his way along the wall of the windowless room, he came to a pile of rubble, evidently the remains of an earlier roof. Working around this, he heard a low mutter of voices and then saw a vague light from the floor. He moved nearer and found himself standing over a trap door, but no ladder descended into the darkness. Yet not far from the opening of the trap was a crack in the ceiling of another room below, and through this opening there now came both light and the sound of voices.

Clarry Jacks was speaking. "Not out there?"

"Duck must be nervous . . . seein' things."

"Well, he knows of this place. He'll come eventually. He'll be looking for me."

"Suppose Lock told him anything?" It was Laramie talking.

"I doubt it. From where I was hid I could see them plain. Lock talked some, all right. I could hear his voice. After Hopalong had the fire goin' I could see them both, and then when light came, Hopalong took off and I knew I had to get down there fast."

"Maybe Lock never saw anything?"

"He saw something, all right. He got a good look at me when the lightning flashed, and he'd know me, mask or no mask."

"You were lucky to run into Harper like you did."

"Yeah. When I spotted them I swung around a hill so I could ride down on them from behind. They were hurryin' to catch Harrington then, and I told 'em I'd chased 'em all the way from town, which accounted for my horse being hard-ridden. Harper knew the tally all right, but Doc never suspected."

Hopalong put his feet through the trap door and lowered himself full length. Then he dropped.

"What was that?" Clarry demanded.

"What?"

"I thought I heard somethin'."

Laramie rose. "Any way into this place but the door?"

"None I can think of. There's a hole in the wall of that upper room. If a feller got on the roof—"

Both men turned like cats. Hopalong Cassidy stood in the dark doorway to the inner room, elbows crooked, his big hands poised above the guns that had ended the career of many an outlaw or professed gunman.

Jacks stared at the hard-boned face, the weather-beaten countenance and blazing eyes, and something turned over within him, something happened that he had never believed could happen to him. His courage seemed to ooze from him. Yet at the height of his terror a thought ran through him, cold and chilling.

He had no choice.

This man had come here hunting him. Despite their elaborate plans, he had come without warning. Jacks uttered a low cry and grabbed for his gun.

Hopalong's crooked, waiting hands flickered, and then the blur ended with stabbing flame. Clarry Jacks, his gun lifting, felt a blow alongside the head and went down. Something else struck him in the side, knocking him to the floor. He hit hard, and his bullet buried itself in the ceiling.

Laramie's gun leaped to his hand, and his first shot grooved the doorjamb where Hopalong stood, and again Cassidy's guns began to flame.

Then suddenly the floor heaved, a wall rippled, and the ceiling caved. From outside there was a wild yell of fear, and wheeling, Hopalong leaped for the door. He lunged into the outer darkness, saw a weird flare of lightning, and beheld the serrated edge of the fault moving against the sky. Stone ground against jagged stone, with an awful sound that turned his bowels to weakness. Hopalong sprang for his remembered escape route.

The next instant a rider charged through the rocking darkness and swung broadside to Hopalong, a gun lifted. Lightning flashed, and Hopalong saw the man was Lock.

"Ben!" he yelled. "It's Cassidy! Get out of here! This fault may close up!"

Lock urged his horse nearer. "Up!" he yelled. "Behind me!"

Laramie charged into the open from the ruins and, seeing Hopalong springing to the horse behind Lock, skidded to a halt and swung up his gun. Ben Lock's long-barreled six-shooter dropped down, and the two guns blasted at almost the same instant. Laramie stepped back, turned half around, and fell full length to the hard-packed earth.

Hopalong felt the powerful muscles of the mustang hunch beneath him, and then they were racing for the outlet of the fault. Another horseman loomed before them. "Hoppy?" The yell was from Shorty Montana.

"Get out!" Cassidy yelled. "Ride, you souwegian!"

The rain was coming down now in torrents, but the earthquake was not over, for after a brief respite it trembled again, and behind them stones cascaded into the fault, roaring long after they were beyond the mouth of the fault. Lightning crackled and rumbled among the distant peaks, and looking for the finger of the granitic upthrust, Hopalong saw nothing. The horizon at that point was empty!

"Swing around," he advised. "My horse is tied back up in the junipers."

"Get Jacks?" Lock asked suddenly.

"Think so. That quake busted things up. He was hit bad and went down just as Laramie opened on me."

"I got that one—dead center."

"It was Jacks who killed your brother."

"I figured that. He or Pony Harper."

"Harper *was* involved somehow—Jacks said something about it while I was hidin' out there in the house."

"I got the feeling," Ben Lock replied, "that he was the one spotting the gold shipments, but I'm not sure."

Hopalong found Topper dragging a picket rope and a branch of the manzanita to which he had been tied. Mounted, he turned toward the ranch. The others fell in beside him.

"Never would have found that place if it hadn't been for you," Lock said suddenly. "I trailed Jacks away from Poker Gap, then lost him. I spotted your tracks, then lost them, but kept the general direction and picked up Jacks's trail again."

Behind them, on the rubble-littered floor of the ruined house, a bloody man groaned, then tried to move. Only the fact that he had partly rolled under the table had saved him from the falling adobe blocks. A bloody furrow lay along his scalp above the ear, and he sat there, blood trickling down his face, staring, shocked and half blind, at the ruin about him, unknowing, uncaring. Lightning showed him the crumpled body of Laramie, and slow curses bubbled at his lips as he remembered the image of that crouched, black-clad man with guns that flamed their death into the room—a man he was going to kill.

Sobbing, Jacks was trying to crawl when Duck Bale felt his way over the ruins. "Take it easy," Bale said. "We Bald Knobbers stick together. I'll get you out of this."

CHAPTER 11

VENGEFUL OUTLAW

It was Tex Milligan who first saw John Gore. He saw him when he was several miles off and kept watch on the lone rider, suspecting at first that it might be Cassidy or Shorty Montana. When he did see who it was, he almost broke a leg getting down the mountain to where Frenchy and Kid Newton were loafing outside the bunkhouse.

Bob Ronson had come from the house at first sign of his descent, and with him were Dr. Marsh and the Ronson sisters.

Before Milligan could burst out with his story, Ronson was alongside him. "Who is it, Tex? What's happened?"

"Gore!" Tex gasped, when he could catch a breath. "John Gore headin' this way. Be here in a couple of minutes. He's ridin' a spent cayuse, and with my glass he looks sore as a boiled owl!"

"He may want peace talk," Ronson said. "If he does, we'll dicker with him." He glanced around the circle of his riders and added quietly, "I'll do the talking."

"Boss," Newton objected, "he may be huntin' trouble. Maybe huntin' me. Let me have him."

"Or me," Ruyters said quietly. "The Kid's had his share of the Gore outfit. I want mine."

"No." Bob Ronson's voice was clear with authority. "I'll handle this, and handle it my way."

The rage of John Gore had now become a cold fire that blazed through every muscle of him. What had happened he had no idea, and strangely, he did not care. Later, when he had calmed down and with time to think, he would have cared, but now he was too filled with a burning lust to vent his fury on someone, something. He had been woefully outgeneraled, and by circumstances, not by men. His trip to Corn Patch had isolated him from the fight when he was most needed; he had been set afoot, trapped in an isolated mountain village with only two dead men for company.

What had happened to his men, he did not know. The deserted ranch, empty of supplies, ammunition, and horses, portended the worst. Certainly, from the look of things, Rocking R men had been on his ranch. Where his men now were, or if any were alive, he did not know. Had he seen them at that moment his fury would have driven him insane, for they were walking, plodding wearily on blistered feet, in boots never made for walking, across the seemingly endless miles of an alkali flat. For all their use to the fight now under way, they might have been on another planet.

John Gore's eyes were red-rimmed from the blazing sun, his face grim under the film of dust, his lips tight with the tenseness of his rage as he rode down the trail and into the yard of the Rocking R.

He had expected to find a deserted ranch and only the horses and perhaps the Ronsons. For Bob Ronson he had only contempt, and for the women only irritation and the hope they would keep out of his way. What he found instead was a small circle of men waiting for him. Frenchy, Tex, Kid Newton—and in the door of the bunkhouse now, Joe Hartley. A few feet away stood another group, the two girls and Doc Marsh. Straight before him was Bob Ronson, who now took a step forward.

"How are you, John?" Ronson spoke clearly. "Get down. I suppose you've come to talk peace."

The word was a red rag to a bull. "Peace!" The fury within him turned his voice hoarse. "I'll peace you, you idiot!"

Ronson was unmoved. He stood quietly, his face white but composed. Frenchy, the oldest hand here, touched his tongue to his lips. Bob Ronson had never faced a situation like this before. Secretly, Frenchy had always been afraid that he would not measure up. More than anything in the world he wanted now to step forward and take this fight off the hands of his boss, but he knew the fierce pride of the young man, knew how much he would resent it. Knowing the others had a like feeling, he whispered, "Stay back. It's his fight."

Ronson said calmly, "Gore, don't be a fool. As we've said before, there is range enough for both of us here. All you have to do is stay on your side of the Blues and not figure because Dad is dead that you can ride roughshod over this range.

"You have no alternative to peace. Your men are out in the desert afoot and pretty badly off from hunger and thirst by now. You have no horses at your ranch nor at any of your stations. Cassidy has seen to that. Harris, with whom you apparently tried to do business, is dead. Within a matter of hours we'll burn Corn Patch to the ground.

"This is an ultimatum. You can make peace now and sign an agreement to remain on your side of the mountains, or we'll ride on the 3 G and burn it to the ground. Then we'll herd your riders, still afoot, out of the country, and you with them!"

Frenchy could scarcely restrain his elation. Cattle Bob in his palmiest days could not have laid it on the line so simply and directly. Frenchy was grinning despite himself, and despite the tightness of the situation.

Gore slid from his horse, so hurried that he staggered when he reached the ground, and then he turned. "I'll see you in hell first!" he roared.

"Sorry, John." Ronson was still cool. "If that's the way you want it."

John Gore was beyond reason. He had never known defeat, and there was nothing in his makeup that would accept it. He knew now only one thing, a red rage and lust to kill. He growled and his hand whipped down for his gun.

To Frenchy that scene moved with the slow pace of a death march. He saw John Gore's flashing draw, not a fast draw as such things go, but much faster than that of Bob Ronson. He saw the rancher's gun come up, heard the hard sharpness of the report, and incredibly Bob Ronson still stood there!

Ronson was lifting his pistol and taking aim at shoulder height, standing sideways as though on a target range. Gore shot again and again. And then Bob Ronson fired.

John Gore's knees buckled and slowly he sank to the ground. From his knees he went over on his face, stretching out on the ground, and there was not a man there but knew he was dead. Slowly, white as death itself, Ronson lowered his pistol.

"Frenchy," he said quietly, "you and the boys put his body in the barn for now. If he is not claimed by some of his own crowd by nightfall, we'll bury him in the morning." He turned then. "Doc, you'd better get your kit. I think I've been shot."

It was pouring rain when Hopalong Cassidy and Shorty Montana rode into the street of Seven Pines. Both men were hungry and badly whipped by the hours of riding. Leaving their horses in the livery stable, they pushed on up the street, their heads buried in their slicker collars, hat brims pulled low. Behind them rode

Ben Lock. He had fallen slightly behind the others, and his face was grim.

"This durned country!" Montana said bitterly. "If she ain't burnin' up with heat, she's drownin' in rain!"

"Let it rain!" Hopalong said. "I'm for a bunk and some blankets. Another few miles and that horse's backbone would have wore clean through to my shirt pockets!"

"What do we do about Harper?" Shorty asked, Hopalong having informed him as to the contents of Thacker's wallet.

"That will wait. We get the Rockin' R trouble off our hands first."

They shook off their dusters and hats on the hotel porch. Inside the dimly lit lobby they paused a moment. A sleepy clerk stuck his head out of his door and glared at them. "Number ten. Pick up the key in the pigeonhole and don't bother me!"

He drew back inside his door but did not return to bed. Instead, he stood thinking for a minute, and then quickly drew on his pants and hurried down the hall to Pony Harper's room.

Harper had been in bed for an hour and was still not asleep. Too many things were happening and there was too little news. He heard the gentle tap on his door and reared up in bed. He reached first for the pistol under his pillow and then listened. The tap came again. "Who is it?" He spoke in a low tone to be heard only just beyond the door.

"Me—Jerry! Got news for you!"

Harper rolled from bed in his flannel nightshirt and opened the door. Jerry came in and closed it quickly behind him. "Figured you'd want to know. Hopalong Cassidy's in town! He and Shorty Montana! Blew in about five minutes ago, and I put 'em in number ten."

"Cassidy? He say anythin'? Any news?"

"Not a word. Both of 'em looked plumb beat, but they sure aren't hurt."

"All right, go to bed. Circulate around in the morning and let me know if you can find out what's been happening."

By morning news had drifted in, as news will. John Gore was dead, killed by, of all people, Bob Ronson! The Gore riders had been trapped, their horses driven off, and they were wandering afoot somewhere in the alkali basin between Willow Springs and the 3 G Ranch. And then, almost an hour later, two men rode into town.

Hankins and Drennan had broken away from the crowd and gone off on their own and had had instant luck. They found some of the horses left by the 3 G grazing in a side canyon. As they had parted under the worst possible terms with the others, neither man felt any necessity of riding back with horses. They mounted bareback and started for Seven Pines.

Their faces were blistered and their feet in terrible shape. Both men were caked with alkali and rifled with only one urgent desire: to get out and stay out.

Hopalong Cassidy was sitting over his second cup of coffee when the two cowhands staggered into Katie's. He looked across the table at them, his blue eyes measuring and cool.

"Coffee's good, boys. What's it to be? Breakfast or trouble?"

Hankins stared sullenly, and it was Drennan who spoke. "Breakfast and a bath. Then a chance to ride on. How about it, Hopalong?"

Shorty Montana's hands were inches from his gun butts, waiting.

"That go with you too, Hankins?" Hopalong asked.

The outlaw nodded sullenly. Then his lips parted in an ironic grin. "You fellers raised hob," he said. "You sure raised hob! If that outfit got to the 3 G without a killin', I'd be surprised. Con was fit to be tied, and that Troy!" He shook his head. "Ah, what a rat! The man's meaner than a crippled coyote, believe me!"

Katie put out coffee for them and then breakfast. While they ate, Shorty Montana sat with his shoulders back against the wall and told them all that had happened. Harris and Dusark dead, John Gore recently killed by Bob Ronson, who was shot but living, and then the biggest news, told for the first time: the killing of Laramie by Ben Lock, and Clarry Jacks by Hopalong Cassidy.

Later that day Hankins and Drennan drifted out of town. Before the end of the week the range had quieted, Corn Patch had been burned out, John Gore had been buried alongside his brother at Seven Pines, and Bob Ronson was slowly recovering from his wound.

Restlessly, Hopalong worked with his outfit, shaping a herd for a drive to market, cleaning water holes, putting in a couple of dams and a drift fence. It was time to leave, and Gibson of the 3 T L would still be watching for him. Yet he stayed on, held by he knew not what. The range war that had blossomed so quickly had died almost as quickly. Nothing was seen of Con Gore, and word came that he had moved his cattle east of the Blues and was running them there.

Rawhide was back in town and was rarely seen away from Pony Harper's side. Sheriff Hadley, moving belatedly to stop the fighting, had repeated the ultimatum laid down by Bob Ronson and had ridden to the 3 G with it. Con Gore had listened in silence and then turned his back and walked into the house. Boucher was still with him, and Troy had hired on as a hand. Of Dud Leeman there was but one report: He had been seen at Unionville but had left town with Duck Bale, no one knew where, not even an idea of where they were going.

One of the last to hear that report was Hopalong Cassidy. Riding in from Mandalay Springs, he was told the story, and back at the Rocking R he sat down on the porch and thought things over.

Dud Leeman had been the riding partner of Clarry Jacks, and the two had been almost inseparable. Duck Bale had been holding the fort at the hideout, and Duck had been alive when they left. Of Laramie there had been no doubt. Hopalong had himself seen the man fall, riddled with bullets. Jacks had fallen, too, but there had been no time to examine him. Under oath Hopalong could not have sworn he was dead.

The peculiar feeling that had disturbed him for the past ten days began to make itself

plain now. Perhaps there had been some unconscious realization that Jacks was not dead,
but alive and a danger. Now he knew that,
whatever else came, he must ride to the hideout and make sure. As long as Clarry was alive,
there would be no peace here. Dangerous before, the man was sure to be utterly vicious
now.

Something of the same feeling seemed to
obsess the men.

"Did either you or Hoppy take a look at
him?" Ruyters was asking. "Maybe Jacks is still
around."

"He was dead all right!" Shorty sounded
too positive. "He sure went down hard with his
head all bloody."

"I've seen men live through some awful
wounds. Remember how Cole Younger rode
away from the Northfield raid, shot through
with bullets?"

"Reminds me." Kid Newton shoved his
narrow-brimmed round hat back on his head.
His boyish face with its few whiskers looked
very young, and only his eyes were those of a
man. "Saw some tracks in that box canyon this
side of Sawtooth. Lone rider, wanderin', sort
of, like he was huntin' something or lookin' the
country over."

"And I saw some over this side the lava

beds," Hartley offered. "Somebody had bedded down near that spring. One man, ridin' a sorrel horse."

It was late afternoon when Hopalong reached Seven Pines. He went at once to Katie's, and she greeted him with a smile. "Seen Ben Lock?" he asked her.

"Yes, he's been around a lot, but he spends most of the time around the High-Grade. He doesn't talk, not even to me, but I think he's watching somebody. Maybe it's Pony Harper."

Hopalong nodded. What did Lock intend to do? It was likely the man did not know himself. Yet a few minutes later, when he saw Harper walk down the street and enter the saloon, he was not sure. Harper looked bad and must have lost fifteen pounds.

"Ben's been riding, too," Katie volunteered. "I don't think he believes Jacks is dead. Do you?"

Hopalong shrugged. "He took one slug, maybe two. Men have lived through lots worse than that. We'll never know unless we go back and look. And that," he added, "is what I think I'll do."

Shorty Montana and Tex Milligan pushed into the room. "How's for some of that coffee, Katie?" Shorty demanded cheerfully. "That cook out at the Rockin' R is good, but he doesn't have your touch with coffee."

"Look, Katie," Milligan interrupted, "I tried to steer Shorty away, but there was no chance. He simply wouldn't go. I know you don't want to lower the tone"—he glanced around smugly—"of your establishment by havin' ornery coyotes around, but I couldn't keep him away."

"Keep me away?" Shorty glared. "Why, you waffle-headed picture of a string bean, you never saw the time you could keep me away from anything! In the first place there isn't enough of you to make a good man! You're so thin you'd have to stand twice in the same place to make a shadow!"

"Huh!" Milligan grunted. "Don't pay him any attention, Katie. He's just sore because he has to stand on his tiptoes to see over a saddle."

Both men were arguing just to hear the sound of their voices, Hoppy knew. While they argued both were acutely conscious of him, and he had a rough idea they were riding herd on him. The thought of it amused him and yet it warmed his heart to think that they liked him enough to worry. That the country was still filled with enemies of the Rocking R and of Hopalong Cassidy, they all knew. Many of the outlaws were gone or had been killed, but others might be lurking about, and some of the ranchers who hoped to profit from the fall of the Rocking R were still sore about their failure.

Con Gore had not been seen in town and had talked to no one. What he was thinking was a complete mystery. That Troy would be nursing a grudge was obvious, and it was probable that Rawhide, who walked always beside Pony Harper, was thinking of his sore feet with no pleasure. It was a rare night that some veiled allusion was not made to his hiking proclivities, and the thing was eating on him, corroding his self-control, and driving him to a fury that was beyond reason.

The sun was scarcely up the following morning before Hopalong forked Topper and headed east for the hideout to settle his doubts once and for all. As on the last occasion when he left the place, the sky was cloudy and it looked like rain. He pushed the white gelding steadily toward the faulted ground, scanning the country with care as he rode. If Jacks was alive, and if he had Dud Leeman and Duck Bale with him, Hopalong might very well be riding into a trap, and a serious one. By now they would know that he had been using the rockslide for a means of entry into the valley, and if they were still there they would certainly be on their guard against that approach.

The lowering clouds pressed down around the higher peaks and in some places had swallowed the serrated crests of the mountains, sinking in cottony billows down the mountainsides and drifting in ghostly wraiths among the scattered junipers. Once, far off, Hopalong saw a coyote lope away and vanish among the greasewood. A tall-eared jackrabbit leaped from its nest in startled confusion and bounded away to lose itself among the sage. All else was still. No breath of air stirred, and the gelding moved steadily and easily through the brush.

Although he kept a close watch, Hopalong spotted no new tracks. Several times he stopped and, squinting his blue eyes against the distance, looked, studied, and examined all within range of his sight. The desert was empty, as far as he could see, no living thing moved or had its being. Soon scattered rocks began to appear, not loose boulders, but the upthrust ledges of the faulted ground. Uneasily he surveyed the prospect, and he did not like it. Getting into the fault canyon would be a serious problem now, and he had to admit to himself that he never approached this place without awe and wonder.

Here there was something far more vast than any work of man. This rock had been broken asunder by the forces of nature itself, a cataclysm that man could not control and before which all his powers, all his inventions were as nothing. The titanic forces that had broken these ledges far beneath the surface of the earth and thrust their jagged edges through the soil were not dead, but lying there only leashed for the time.

The land was still. A silence lay upon it, a vaster silence than the desert usually knew. No cicada sang in this cloudy weather; no bird twittered among the greasewood. All was still, and with the stillness his alertness grew, his readiness for the danger he seemed to sense.

Topper slowed to a walk, ears pricked forward. Occasionally, of his own volition, he stopped and looked ahead and around. There was upon the earth a feeling of expectation, a sense of waiting. Uneasily, Hopalong shook off the feeling. He was a man not easily disturbed, yet the last one to shake off such a feeling as of no importance. It remained only for him to interpret it, and do so correctly and at once.

Much of this might be his own imagination, his own mind. Tough and practical as he was, he still retained strong respect for the wild. There were strange currents of feeling in the wilderness, or perhaps those feelings were in men when they were in the wilds. In any event, most men who have lived in the great loneliness of Arctic, desert, ocean, or high mountains but have known that peculiar feeling that conveys itself to all who inhabit the wilderness.

Over such country as this he had ridden much of his life. He knew its moods and changes, and at the same time he knew that sixth sense that sometimes warns of danger. He had never, so far as he could recall, underrated an opponent. If Clarry Jacks was alive, he was a deadly antagonist, a man cold-nerved but fired with killing lust, and one not easily upset by trifles. He would be a hard man to kill, and he might take someone with him when he went.

The rockslide was seemingly unchanged, but the serrated ridge showed many differences, and the towering upthrust of granite appeared to have fallen inward. Hopalong again descended to the bottom.

He had detected no sign of life about either part of the fault canyon, and now on the bottom he saw that the adobe house was a ruin. Two walls stood, but both were cracked. No horses remained in the corrals. If Clarry Jacks was alive, Hopalong Cassidy was sure he was not in the canyon.

The floor of the canyon was a jumble of fallen rock, and around the base of the walls the earth was broken and shoved back by the movement of the rock. A silence as of death hung over the place, an eerie loneliness that brought an involuntary shudder to his shoulders. Among the ruins of the house he found no sign of a body, although the darkness of blood was on the floor. Then near the corral he found a grave.

LARAMIE
1881
DIED WITH HIS BOOTS ON

One grave! Clarry Jacks was alive! Swiftly now Hopalong moved to the shack where he had originally talked with Bale. Here there was every evidence of hurried leave-taking. Glancing at the gelding, Hopalong saw the horse had his ears up and was looking wildly about. Warily, Hopalong looked around him, and then the landscape seemed to shimmer.

Cassidy reached the saddle in one long dive and swung up as the startled horse leaped into a dead run for the canyon mouth. Under the horse's feet the earth seemed to groan, and with an appalling grinding the rock to the south pushed higher and higher into the sky. With the portals of the narrow opening seeming even narrower than usual, Hopalong lunged the horse through. Beside him the earth cracked and there was a vile odor as of sulfur mingled with something long dead, and then the horse was down the draw and into the open. The effects of the quakes were noticeable even here, for long cracks ran into the desert as far as he could see. Turning at right angles, he ran Topper out of the faulted area, slowed to a canter, then a walk.

Clarry Jacks was alive. If so, where was he? Corn Patch had been burned to the ground, and while he might have ridden to join the remnants of the 3 G crowd, Hopalong doubted it. Jacks was a man to lead, not follow. Duck Bale would be with him, and by now he would be in communication with Dud Leeman.

Cutting the desert for some sign of the outlaws would be useless. If they were to be tracked it would be with the mind, not the sign they would leave upon the desert. Dud and Clarry had both been known around Unionville, yet he doubted they would go there for that very reason. Hopalong believed that

Clarry would hope his enemies would accept his death as a fact.

Night was coming on. A cluster of cottonwoods in a hollow raised the possibility of water, and Hopalong started the white gelding toward them. He suddenly realized he was tired, and he could tell by the way Topper was walking that the horse was also. The cottonwoods did not prove themselves liars, for among them was a small pool supplied by a seep. The manzanita clustered thick at one end of the grove, and there Hopalong made camp alongside a huge deadfall. Nothing bigger than a coyote could possibly get through the manzanita without making noise enough to wake the dead, and the log offered some cover in the other direction. Scraping together some bark fragments, some dead branches, and a few chunks of half-rotted wood, Hopalong got his fire going, a small fire that threw very little light.

He was pouring coffee when he heard a hoof click on stone, and he put down his cup, then rolled over into the brush near the big end of the log, rifle in hand. For a long time there was no sound, and he eyed the steaming coffee irritably. Somebody would have to come up on him just as the coffee was hot!

An idea occurred to him, and with utmost

caution he snaked out the rifle barrel, hooking the front sight through the handle of the cup, and slowly dragged it back toward him. Luckily it slopped over very little, and it was with real satisfaction that he gulped the hot coffee. Now let them come. He was ready.

Again a hoof clicked, closer this time. Whoever it was approaching had become mighty cautious. Hopalong studied the skyline, seeking some obstruction that would blot out the stars, but there was none. A murmur of voices came to his ears, and he tilted his head, trying to catch the inflection. When it came to him he grinned, and easing around the end of the log, he crawled forward through the grass. When he could see their broad hats stark against the sky, he said aloud, "If you pilgrims would holler when you approach a camp, you wouldn't get caught this way."

Shorty and Tex turned sheepishly as he walked from the brush. "We sort of figured you might want company," Tex suggested.

"And as long as we're ridin' down the country we figured to bring you the news."

"What news?" Hopalong demanded suspiciously.

"Well, Doc and Miss Irene are gittin' hitched up real soon."

"I knew that."

"And there was a shindig of some sort over to the 3 G. Hank Boucher got into an argument with Con Gore, and that coyote Troy up and shot Boucher in the back. Doc figures he may pull out of it, but it's still a question."

"That outfit can't even get along with themselves," Hopalong said. "Come on back to camp—coffee's hot." As they started back he turned his head. "Feel that quake?"

"Feel it?" Tex said. "Scared the livin' daylights out of me. Caught us right out on the open desert, nothin' close up, but we could see rocks fallin' off the ridges. That old flat-top mesa south of here lost a corner."

Over coffee Hopalong recounted the experiences of the day and the finding of Laramie's grave. He also commented on the fact that he believed Jacks was alive and teamed up with Bale and Leeman.

"We heard he was alive. Ben Lock cut the sign of that toed-in paint you trailed before the stage robbery. There was three horses in the bunch, all with riders. He followed 'em some distance before he lost 'em. Feller came in the other day said they stopped him on the road. He never said a word about it until Lock told us. The three of them spooked him so bad he was afraid to talk, but he said that they stopped him on the road and made him give them some grub."

"Where do you think he'll head for?" Milligan asked.

"No tellin'. Maybe that claim on Star Peak."

"Doubt it," Montana objected. "Too many people know about it now. Although there's old tunnels around what's left of Star City, and there's shelter there. That might be it."

"If I was him," Tex said, "I'd hit northwest toward the Black Sand. I'd lose myself in those hills over yonder."

"Well"—Hopalong shrugged—"if he gets out of the country I won't follow him. It's time I was movin' on, anyway."

Tex fed a few sticks into the fire and started a long story about running cattle down on the Brazos, and in a few minutes he and Shorty were arguing hotly over respective methods of roping and whether it was better to tie or dally the rope.

Hopalong leaned back and listened with only half his attention. It would be good to see Red Connors now. The last time he had seen Johnny or Mesquite was down on the Gila. They had come along then and butted into a fight just in time to help him. That had always been the way of the Bar 20 or any of the outfits started by the old crowd: They never hesitated to side each other.

He grinned, remembering the fights Mesquite and he had found themselves getting into at Dodge and Ogallala, but even those towns weren't what they had been. The old cattle drives weren't so big as they used to be, either. It was towns like Tombstone and Deadwood that were getting all the play now. But for sheer murderous toughness there were a half-dozen mining camps in Utah and Nevada that would compare with the old trail towns. The longhorn had taken over from the buffalo and now was giving way to the white-face. Before long there would be plows on the range. The old West was changing, and there was nothing to do but accept it.

"What now?" Shorty asked suddenly. "You goin' to hunt Jacks?"

"Possibly." Cassidy rolled a smoke and stretched his legs to ease the cramp building in his thighs. "But it could be he's had enough. As for the 3 G, I hope they mind their own affairs. Ronson wants no trouble he can avoid." His eyes twinkled. "And I'm feelin' about the same."

Milligan looked downcast. "Just when it was gettin' to be a good fight, too!"

.   .   .

In 1863, Unionville had been wide open. At that time it had ten stores, six hotels, nine saloons, two express offices, two drugstores, four livery stables, and a brewery. Everybody had a claim staked out and every claim was potentially the richest ever found. Men without a nickel to their name talked in terms of thousands of dollars, and they exchanged, bought, or sold claims, and veins that sold by the foot. Mining men being what they are, optimism was the normal attitude, and it takes an optimistic man to live in a dugout or brush shelter while grubbing in a mountainside for the rainbow's end; but in a country where a chunk of silver nearly a ton in weight had been found and rich veins were paying off in millions, optimism had some excuse for being.

Within twenty miles of Unionville a half dozen hamlets were born, some to last only a few months, some a few years, and some to move at least once during their lifetimes. One of these was Star City, a haphazard collection of habitations clustered on a mountainside guarded from view by a lower but neighboring peak.

There had been a rich strike here. It had lasted almost two years, then died. The miners, finding too little to do, had drifted on to Unionville and elsewhere. The shacks remained, and in them a few optimists and a few casual squatters. The optimists stayed on, while the squatters changed from week to week. At last even these drifted on and the town acquired a few desert owls, a pack rat or two, and some migrating bats.

Clarry Jacks was white-faced and half dead when the faithful Duck Bale brought him to the collection of shacks. In one of these that was reasonably intact they found shelter, and Bale, whose experience with gunshot wounds had been wide, worked over the injuries. The scalp had been laid open to the bone and there had been a concussion, but the body wound was the most serious. After a few days, when he could leave the wounded man without danger, Bale made contact with Dud, then returned to the cluster of shacks.

For a week Jacks hovered between life and death, ministered to by Bale himself and by old Doc Benton, smuggled into the town blindfolded by Dud Leeman. Benton, a former army surgeon now far gone in liquor, still retained ability, and he used it. When he finally was returned to the saloons of Unionville, Jacks was well on the way to recovery. Yet as he recovered, his manner grew increasingly irritable, then vicious.

Moving from Star City, they took shelter in the half-dozen ramshackle buildings in a deep gash in the mountainside that constituted all that remained of the High Card Mining Company. Thin, white-faced, and mean, Clarry Jacks paced the floor, seething with repressed fury. Duck Bale watched him and worried, and even the phlegmatic Dud Leeman eyed him with misgivings. Whether it was the sharp defeat administered by Hopalong or the concussion was hard to say. The fact remained that the man's character stood starkly revealed now. The cloak of easy laughter was gone, and all that remained was the killer, but now without a single relieving virtue.

Dud Leeman chewed silently on his plug of tobacco and ruminated upon what he knew of his companion. Clarry Jacks had been close to him, but Clarry Jacks in a tight spot had murdered Dakota Jack. Dud had known for a long time that Vasco Graham and Jacks were one. It had been Bale, a friend of Jacks back in his Bald Knob days, who had told him the truth. None of it made Dud any more confident of his future.

"My idea," he ventured once, "would be

to pull out. This country's finished as long as Cassidy's here. We can take care of Pony later."

"Forget that!" Jacks whirled on him, his eyes narrowed viciously. "We don't leave this country until both Cassidy and Harper are dead! I want that gold, but that isn't so important to me as gettin' Cassidy!"

"Boss," Leeman protested quietly, "the whole country's against us now. If we stay we haven't got a chance to get out alive. I mean it. We can get away now. They don't know whether you're alive or dead, but believe me, they are gettin' suspicious.

"Cassidy," he continued, "is ridin' the country. So's Ben Lock, and from all I hear, it was Lock who killed Laramie. Yesterday, from the top of the ridge, I watched Lock for two hours with a glass. He was on a trail. Maybe it was yours—I don't know. Anyway, he lost it down in the valley, but every so often he'd look up and see these mountains and study 'em like he figured on scoutin' around. I tell you, Clarry, Lock isn't quittin'!"

Jacks's eyes were somber with hatred. "What's the matter, Dud?" he sneered. "Gettin' yellow? I wouldn't be surprised if it was Bale here, but you!"

He turned on his heel and walked to the door, but when he looked back he said, low-voiced and tense with emotion: "Nobody leaves me! Get that? Nobody!"

He stalked outside, and they heard his steps receding down the trail. White-faced, Bale glanced at Dud. "He sure has changed."

Leeman nodded worriedly. "There's no sense in stayin', Duck! None at all! I tell you, that Lock is like a bloodhound. He'll never leave that trail! That hombre worries me, stickin' at it the way he does. He's lost weight, he's slept out for days, but he keeps goin'. He'll never quit. As for Hopalong, I'd sooner tackle a catamount in his own cave than that hombre. The only reason Clarry is alive today is because of that quake."

"What you goin' to do?" Bale inquired cautiously.

Dud Leeman said nothing. He got swiftly and silently to his feet and peered outside, then sat down. "Do?" he said loudly. "I'm stickin' with the boss. What else? It's just a matter of how we can get that Cassidy hombre!"

Bale looked at him quickly, then at the window, and nodded. "Yeah," he said, "the first thing is to get him, then that gold from Harper."

Clarry Jacks stalked into the room suddenly and glared sullenly first at one, then at the other. That he had gone down the trail, then dodged back to listen, they both knew. Jacks lighted a cigarette, drew impatiently on it, then stalked again to the door, muttering to himself.

Dud Leeman looked at his broad back, then shot a quick glance at Duck. It was not in him to shoot a man in the back, but at that moment he wondered if it would not be best. It was beginning to look like the only choice they had was to kill or be killed.

Clarry Jacks turned around and stared at them, his eyes malevolent and evil, and behind that there was something else that Dud Leeman glimpsed for the first time and recognized with a chill. Clarry Jacks was insane.

CHAPTER 12

FURTIVE ENEMY

A week later Hopalong rode into town, accompanied by Tex and Shorty. They had searched the ruins of Star City and found nothing. What might have been the remains of a campfire had been scattered, and it was impossible to tell if the charred sticks found on the spot were a few days or a few months old. Nobody had seen either Dud Leeman or Duck Bale.

Pony Harper was never alone. Rawhide haunted his vicinity; his dark eyes with their yellowish whites were always busy, searching, staring, watching windows, doorways, and alleys. Harper had grown noticeably thin. His jowls, which had been plump, now sagged over his heavy jawbones. He was irritable and seldom in the High-Grade during rush hours.

Ben Lock had returned to town and, despite Katie's objections, had bought supplies and started out again. He had admitted that he was having no luck but was working systematically now, searching each section of country as though hunting strays or prospecting. Rumors got around. Clarry Jacks was alive—somebody who knew somebody else was told by his cousin that Jacks had been seen. Jacks, according to another story, was dead. He had been buried by moonlight in Poker Gap, dying of wounds.

Ben Lock met Hoppy in the livery stable at Seven Pines. Hopalong had just come in and Lock was leaving. "Cut any sign, Ben?"

Lock shrugged. "Not lately. He's alive, though. I got a feelin'."

"Yeah." Hopalong sat down on a bale of hay and struck a match with his thumbnail. "A man's got to figure this thing with his head. No real trail. You just got to think it out."

"Never was much good at that," Ben said. "I can read trail sign as good as most men, and I can follow a color upstream, but that about lets me out." He looked at Hopalong thoughtfully. "What do you reckon he'll do, Hoppy?"

"Hard to say," Cassidy admitted. "But let's take it for granted that Duck and Leeman are with him. That means three men. They have to have food, water, ammunition, and concealment. Ammunition they probably have without buyin' more. Maybe not, but we'll figure it that way. Now that still means they have to have food, water, and a hideout.

"He's not in Seven Pines—you can bank on that. North of here the country is nearly all Rockin' R, with the only water on our range. We've rebuilt the cabin at Willow Springs and the boys are there every other day or so. Mandalay, Haystack, and the Rabbithole likewise are visited. Corn Patch was burned to the ground and would be too risky for 'em.

"Clarry has enemies in Unionville, so he'll stay away from there. Poker Gap in the daytime is wide open. What does that leave us?"

"Not much," Ben admitted, scowling. He looked around quickly at the sound of a step and saw Tex Milligan and Shorty Montana. Both were looking at the map sketched in the dirt of the floor.

Shorty dropped to his haunches. "Say, Ben," he asked, "when you were lookin' around Star City, did you go to the High Card Mine?"

"Where's that?"

Shorty indicated on the map. "Deep canyon back in there. If you didn't know she was there, you could sure miss it."

"No," Ben admitted. "I reckon that's one I missed. Water there?"

"Uh-huh. Not very good, but water."

Ben nodded seriously. "Then that could be it. I'm headin' that way." He turned to look at Hopalong. "Want to come along, Cassidy?"

Cassidy shook his head regretfully. "Sorry. I got to get out to the ranch and see Ronson. Anyway," he added, "I've had my trouble with Clarry Jacks. As long as he leaves the R alone, I'll leave him alone, unless he starts something."

Nevertheless, he was worried. Knowing something of the caliber of man Clarry Jacks was, he realized that so long as the man was alive and in the Seven Pines country there would be trouble. It was time he himself moved on. He was restless and wanted to head north for Gibson's spread. There was only a little business with Ronson to hold him now. Yet somehow he hesitated to go, and itching with irritation, he paused on the street and studied it without seeing anything before him.

It was a long time since anything had bothered him this much, for usually he was a man immune to petty irritations and not one inclined to pay attention to hunches, but right now he had a feeling that trouble was headed his way. Gloomily he watched Ben Lock saddle up and strike out across the valley toward Poker Gap and the hills beyond. Shorty and Tex were in the High-Grade enjoying a drink, and he sat down on the edge of the boardwalk.

Hopalong was scowling at his own uncertainty, and it was not like him to feel as he did. Yet he knew the kind of man Clarry Jacks was, and it worried him that the man was still at large. His eyes drifted along the boardwalk across the street where two old men sat in the sun, spinning yarns of the old days in the Mother Lode country. Beyond them, in the door of the High-Grade, Pony Harper stood, his coat hanging a little slack these days. Rawhide came to the door and reported something to Harper.

Hopalong's eyes keened as they saw the reaction. Harper stiffened, then leaned forward, asking a question. Rawhide replied, then gestured off to the west, and the two talked excitedly. Watching with interest, Hopalong wondered what could have them so excited. Then they left the porch and went around to the side of the saloon, where they examined the ground and the window ledge. Suddenly noticing him, Harper straightened and said something in a low tone to Rawhide, who immediately glanced over at Hopalong Cassidy. Then both men walked inside.

Thoroughly interested now, Hopalong waited until they were out of sight. Then he

crossed the street and examined the ground under the window. The tracks were plain enough,
for here a man with small booted feet had
stood and tried to force up a window. The
marks on the ledge of the window and its frame
were obvious enough. That he had not suc-
ceeded was equally obvious.

Clarry Jacks had been in town!

If he had tried to force a way in through
the office window of the High-Grade, it must
have been after hours, for the saloon was open
until two o'clock almost every night. Where,
then, had he gone? And why had he tried to get
into the High-Grade?

Returning to his horse, Hopalong stood
for a while with his hand on the pommel, studying the matter. And then another idea came to
him and his eyes shifted. He stared thoughtfully at Jaeger's store, which was separated
from the High-Grade by only a few feet. Old
Fritz Jaeger, a thin, cantankerous man, slept in
the back of his store. Had he heard anything?
Hopalong dropped the reins over the hitch
rack again and tied a slipknot. Then he turned
and walked across to the store.

Jaeger looked up at Hopalong, then came
toward him. "Something for you?"

"Yeah. Some .44s. Give me two boxes."
While the old man went back of the counter for

the shells, Hopalong looked around. It was the typical western store. Down the center was a counter covered with merchandise, mostly clothing of various types for both men and women. A counter ran around the store on three sides, and the walls behind were shelved to the ceiling and lined with goods—all that a man might need or think of needing for living on the range. Tools, nails, rifles, ammunition, knives, rope, buckets, tubs, and all manner of food supplies.

Jaeger placed the two boxes of shells on the counter before Hopalong and then looked up at him. Something in the cold eyes made him vaguely uneasy. "You sleep in the back of the store?" Hopalong inquired casually.

Jaeger stiffened. "Yeah. Anything more? If not, I got work to do."

"It can wait." Hopalong's eyes had chilled slightly. "Hear anything last night after you went to bed? Or this morning, say after two?"

"What would I hear?" Jaeger asked impatiently. His eyes avoided Hoppy's. "High-Grade closes up at two sharp. By the end of thirty minutes this here town is like a grave."

Hopalong's eyes roved about the store, then fell on a box filled with chisels. He picked one up and studied it carefully. Unless he was much mistaken, it was such a chisel that had been used to try to force the window of the High-Grade office. The width was the same, the— He glanced up suddenly and caught the wary, fearful expression in Jaeger's eyes. "Sold a chisel like this lately?"

"No." Jaeger fumbled for words. "Can't remember as I have."

"Sell one last night? Or have one taken from you?"

"No! I was closed last night! I close early! If I had, don't you figure I'd tell you?"

"You might, and then again maybe you mightn't. If you did, you'd better tell me."

Jaeger was silent, his eyes narrowing, his jaw set stubbornly. "If I did," he said irritably, "it would be my own business! Now, if you aren't wantin' anythin' else, I'll go."

"Jaeger"—Hopalong's voice chilled—"I'm a right friendly man. I'd like to stay that way if you let me. From now on, the Rockin' R and the mines will be your big customers, as they used to be. The Gores are goin' to talk mighty small now, and Clarry Jacks is through. You'd better make up your mind where you stand."

"And get shot for it?" Jaeger snarled.

"Possibly. That's a chance an honest man has to take sometimes. I'll tell you something,

Jaeger. If you had a visitor last night, I'm goin' to know it. If you don't tell me, Jaeger, and if you don't side with honest folks, then you better figure on closin' up shop and leavin'."

Jaeger hesitated, his eyes ugly with hatred. "All right," he said bitterly. "Jacks was here last night. He woke me up, bought ammunition and a new rifle. Then he picked up one of those chisels and told me if I knew what was good for me I'd keep shut about what I heard and saw. Then he tried to bust open a window on the High-Grade but she was nailed shut, so he gave up when some riders came into the street."

"Was he alone?"

"No, there was two hombres with him. Maybe more. Only one I saw was Dud Leeman. He come in with Jacks and stood by the front window watchin' the street."

"What else did he get?"

"Grub and stuff. Quite a lot of it." Jaeger stared at Hopalong. "That all you want to know?"

"Where did he go when he left here?"

"How should I know?" Jaeger demanded angrily. "I don't watch folks that come here. I don't know where he went, and I don't want to know. As long as he leaves me alone, I don't care what he does."

Hopalong Cassidy walked outside and dropped to a seat on the edge of the walk. Scowling, his hat shoved back on his head, he studied the situation. Wherever Jacks had been, he was evidently on the move now and had something in mind. It was not likely he would leave the country, for he was not the sort to run away. Defeat would rankle, and he would need to win at least a minor victory before leaving, if he left at all.

Yet the fact that he had tried to force an entry into the office of the saloon meant that he was not on friendly terms with Pony Harper, and that could account for Harper's very obvious worry. However, what Jacks would need now would be a hiding place, and a new one.

Hopalong looked up as a shadow fell across him. It was Katie. Her face was white and worried. "Hoppy, Con Gore's up at the restaurant. He wants to talk to you."

"All right." Hopalong hitched his guns around under his hands. "How'd he act?"

"Well, all right, I guess," Katie replied. "At least he didn't seem to be looking for trouble. When I told him I wanted no trouble in my place, he said that was why he chose it, because he didn't think you'd start anything there."

Hopalong Cassidy fell in beside the girl, and they walked toward the café. Stopping on the walk before the restaurant, Hopalong opened the door carefully with his left hand. He stepped swiftly through the door and faced Gore, who sat at the opposite end of the room. The big hard-faced ex-convict nodded. "Howdy, Cassidy! Come and sit!"

Cassidy walked slowly across the room, then drew back a chair and dropped astride of it. "What is it, Con?"

The big man hesitated, then looked up, his face flushed with embarrassment. "This here don't set so well some ways, Cassidy," he said, "but I'm makin' peace talk. I don't want any more trouble."

"That makes sense," Hopalong agreed. "I don't want any either."

Gore was relieved. "You figure that'll go with Ronson?" he asked. "I reckon we were wrong. Windy talked John and me into this scrap. Not that I'm blamin' him. I was just as bad. We figured that, with the Old Man dead, Ronson would quit. He had more sand than we figured on. We asked for trouble and we got it —more than we wanted."

"What about your outfit? What about Troy? He's a bad one, Con."

"Yeah." Con's lips tightened. "I guess you needn't worry about him. He's out of it." Gore hesitated, then added, "I'm not so much. I've done time, and I've killed my man, but when Hank and I had that trouble, Troy had no call to butt in an' shoot him in the back."

"What happened?"

"Well, I give him his choice. To hit the saddle and slope it, or reach for a gun. He was mighty nasty, but he went and saddled up. Then he grabbed iron when he figured my back was turned. I was watchin' him and—well, I beat him to it."

"All right," Hopalong said briefly. "I've talked this over with Ronson. Your cattle can run east of the Blues—and west of them, as long as you acknowledge that they are on Rockin' R range. The only thing we don't go for, Con, is somebody tryin' to shove us off. There's water and grass for all, but it's got to be for all. That clear?"

Gore was relieved. "Sure is, an' mighty fair. I always did hear you was fair and square." He shoved back his chair and got up.

Hopalong watched as Gore walked away. That was an issue well closed, but there was still Clarry Jacks, and he was the worst of them all—the man really to be feared. That such was the case was obvious from the actions of Pony Harper. If ever Hopalong had seen a man driven by worry and fear, it was Harper.

The man had no stamina, no real courage. He was a big, smooth, easy-talking man, the kind who could plan, think, and weave a plot, and one who would not hesitate at murder if it could be done without danger to himself, but there was no real bottom to the man. He was an empty shell. Behind him Clarry Jacks loomed like something bigger, stronger, more dangerous. In gun skill the fellow definitely ranked among the best, but there was that something else about him that disturbed Hoppy.

That Jacks was insane, he had not guessed, although he had wondered a little. That Jacks had no plan to leave the country was obvious from his actions, for he could have been long gone by now. Hoppy went to the kitchen and refilled his cup of coffee and took it to a table where Harrington sat.

The mining man looked up. "Howdy, Hoppy! Sit down, will you?"

"Yeah." Hoppy tried his coffee and placed the cup back on the table. "Clarry Jacks was in town last night."

Harrington's eyes were startled. "In town? Here?"

"Uh-huh. You know this country well?"

"Sure. Lived here as a kid, then went back east to school. I worked around the country, then finally came back. What's on your mind?"

"Jacks. Nobody'll be safe as long as he's around. I don't like huntin' a man, but he's mean and he isn't leavin' the country."

"Lock will find him."

"In time, but there isn't much time. Harper's scared of every movement now. He jumps when he sees his shadow. Rawhide walks like he was on eggshells. What I want to know, where could a man hide? He's got grub, he's got ammunition, but he'll need water and a place where he can't be stumbled into. My guess would be he isn't far from here."

"You know most of the water holes yourself." Harrington rubbed his jaw. The fact that Jacks was alive and around worried him. He needed money and was planning a big shipment. "North of here, the Rockin' R outfit has the range well covered; he'd never find a hideout there. South, the country is too open, and there are too many passes through the mountains and too much travel. East is the country you know, the ruins of the Patch, Unionville, Star City."

"He was up in there," Hopalong said. "I

think he's left those mountains for some place closer. My idea is that he's plannin' a strike. What about west of here?"

"Well," Harrington said slowly, "there's the Black Sand Desert, narrow to the northwest, not any water until you get across."

"Too far. What about further south?"

Harrington studied the problem. "Due west of here," he said, "are the lava beds. I don't know. You couldn't walk a hundred yards into them without risk. There's lava rock bubbles—thin as glass, some of them. A wrong step and you go right through. And the rock is sharp as razors. Cut a man's shoes to nothing."

"No water?"

"Yes, there's water on the edge. East and just a shade north of here, there's a spring. Follow the edge of the beds and you couldn't miss it. So far as anybody knows, there's nothing back there. The stretch is about ten miles along and two to three miles wide, with some good peaks among 'em."

After Harrington had gone, Hopalong sat over his second cup and studied the situation. The more he considered it, the more he thought the lava beds were the place. A man could always come out of them for water, or there might be water back inside. Down in New

Mexico there were some lava beds, with numerous little hollows where there was water, grass, and even trees, although a man might wander for days and never find even one of them if he did not know where to look. Such a place, if one existed in this lava bed, would make an ideal hideout.

The next morning Hopalong was not surprised to find Ben Lock sitting over a cup of coffee at Katie Regan's.

"Shorty was right," he said. "They were at the High Card mine but they pulled out days ago."

Hopalong strolled closer and sat down. "I've got an idea. Want to hear it?"

"Anything. I'm fresh out."

Ben grinned at Katie as she refilled his cup. "Reckon my time's short around here," Ben said. "You ever think about livin' in the mountains, Katie?"

"It wouldn't be a bad place to live," Katie agreed noncommittally. "I've thought about a lot of places."

"When I come back from this hunt, I reckon I'm goin' home. Maybe I'll be goin' alone, maybe not."

Hopalong grinned as he lifted his cup, and he caught Katie looking at him suspiciously. He winked, then said, "Nobody ought to be alone in the mountains. Not for long, anyway. A man needs company."

"What are you two gettin' at?" Katie demanded, concealing her smile. "Talkin' in riddles." She started for the kitchen, then hesitated. "Anybody who has any ideas about livin' in the mountains should start for them right soon. A man can wait too long. He can go to the well too often."

CHAPTER 13

FINISH FIGHT

From the kitchen came the sputter of eggs in the pan. Hopalong studied Lock. He was a clean-cut, handsome young man under his stubble of beard. His clothes were worn but clean, and he had gravely humorous gray eyes that regarded the world with a thoughtful amusement and understanding. Katie, he reflected, could do a lot worse.

"What's on your mind?" Lock demanded. "Was it about Jacks?"

Hopalong explained the theory he had concocted from his talk with Harrington. "Now," he added, "it may be a wild guess, but he might be there. My idea is to ride over and see what's what. But there may be some hombres friendly to him around town, so we'd better be mighty careful and not leave town together."

Hopalong Cassidy took the trail to the Rocking R, but only three miles out of town the trail dropped into a gulch, and Hopalong took this opportunity to turn the gelding up the bank and into the junipers. From there he angled under cover of the trees, across a long slope to the crest of the ridge, going over it swiftly and descending into a hollow beyond. At the head of steep-walled Mule Canyon there was a perfect view of the lava beds, which were not five miles away. Heat waves danced in the air, but from this altitude, with his glass, a fair view of the black sea of lava could be had. Several peaks towered above the lava, their shoulders black with it, but they gave promise of water within the beds themselves. From this distance the area looked black and gloomy, and Hopalong could well understand the feelings of the people who avoided the beds. Moreover, there could be no earthly reason for anyone approaching them, which would be all the better for Clarry Jacks.

Ben Lock was waiting for him at the mouth of Mule Canyon. He got to his feet, grinning, as Hoppy rode up. "Made it, I see." He jerked his head over his shoulder toward the lava beds. "Miserable-lookin' place. I reckon we're goin' to find our man."

"Likely." Hopalong squatted by the small fire Lock had built. The dry sticks of greasewood made no smoke. "Move across tonight and hide out somewhere on the edge of the bed."

"Yeah. They'll be watchin' by day." Lock looked quizzically at Hoppy. "That Katie's quite a gal, ain't she?"

Hopalong chuckled. "Well, she makes the best coffee around here. If I were you I'd stake that claim quick."

Lock scowled. "I hear Shorty's pretty thick with her."

"A man can hear anything!" Hoppy turned his head toward the strip of blackness that was the lava beds. "Pay no attention."

The day drew on and the sun lowered itself in a great red ball above the lava beds. The shadows grew long and the sunlight faded and left purple mountains behind. A nighthawk swept by, darting swiftly about in pursuit of some insect. Hopalong got up and saddled Topper.

"Give it twenty minutes," he said, "with the background of these mountains, and they couldn't see us until we were well out in the open."

At last they moved out, neither man in a talkative mood. The first stars were appearing before they had gone a mile, and for luck Hopalong changed course suddenly, heading farther north. If they had been seen and it was believed they were headed for the lava beds, the change of course would make it impossible for a trap to be laid for them.

At a few minutes before ten o'clock they watered their horses at the spring, then withdrew them into a grassy notch in the lava, where they were partly concealed. Lock clambered up on the lava and stared off across the waste. It was wild and lonely, impossibly beautiful, like some landscape on the moon. Jagged ridges of lava, then rolling swells like a vast ocean frozen into instant rigidness. No tree, no shrub, no blade of grass, only the rolling, dull black rock, yet edged and spined like broken glass.

Lock stared gloomily over the lava, remembering Jesse. Jesse had always loved the wild country. Then he was shot down when his life was scarcely begun! Behind him Cassidy mounted the rock, and they stood together, the comforting of the hard-bitten gunfighter sensed only in his quiet presence.

"They'll be here," Cassidy said, nodding. "Somewhere out there they've found a spot. We know that Jacks is really Vasco Graham and that he ran through this country with Dakota Jack, who knew it better than the Piutes."

Ben Lock nodded, looking into the distance. "Yeah, but where?"

Hopalong nodded toward the nearest peak. "We'll try that area. There'll be drainage off that peak, perhaps some subirrigation. At the foot of the mountain there'll be water, the chances are. Anyway, it's a place to start."

Lock lifted his hand suddenly. "Listen!"

Hopalong listened for a long moment, and then the shrill yapping of a coyote sounded someplace behind them, and then, faint and far away, the blows of an ax!

"It's out there," he agreed. "They must have wood, but where would they get it back in there? Could be a water hole and some trees."

"Yes."

Lock threw down his cigarette. "Hoppy," he said quietly, "a man never knows what comes next. Perhaps I'm slated to get mine this time. Those boys are rugged. If anything happens to me, you get that Jacks for me, will you?"

"Somebody's got to," Hopalong agreed. "The man's runnin' mad."

"And tell Katie—" Ben's voice slowed and stopped. Then he shrugged. "Aw, the dickens with it! I'll tell her myself!"

Cassidy chuckled. "Sure. I knew that."

Lock looked at the gunfighter curiously. "Hoppy, don't you ever worry about cashin' in? You don't show it."

Hopalong shrugged. "I reckon not. When it comes it will come. I don't think about this fate business. I just ride along, take no chances I don't have to take, and what happens will happen."

The morning sun was a pale half-moon over the lava beds when their fire was warming. Lock put coffee on, and Hopalong wandered out into the desert to pick up some dried bits of greasewood and juniper.

The smell of the fire was good, and the coffee was better. Lock rubbed the sleep from his eyes and shivered against the morning chill. "Got to be a way in there," he said. "We'll have to scout for it."

Hopalong considered the situation. "No telling which way it'll be, either. This lava could have stopped anywhere. Looks like the flow was split by one of those peaks, so there could be an open space between the two halves. Might be only a few feet wide; mightn't be there at all. It's durned treacherous stuff, too.

There's bubbles in it. The top is thin as an egg-shell, some of 'em. You step on one and the next thing you're lyin' in the bottom of a hole and nobody is goin' to find you. You'll have to carry a stick and tap on the rock with it. See if she sounds hollow."

"They never crossed the lava."

"Maybe not, but if we slip up on 'em, we might have to."

While Lock saddled the horses Hoppy kicked out the fire and obliterated all signs of it. He mounted, then turned. "You ride north," he said, "and I'll head south. If you find an opening, step out in the desert and set up a cairn. I'll do the same."

Ben Lock mounted. "Okay. Luck!" he said, and moved away along the swell of the lava.

Hopalong turned south. The lava here was a wall, like a lofty parapet with black blocks and cubes of lava rock scattered at its base. Then this wall gave way to a black swell like a frozen wave, corrugated and cruel. For over an hour he drifted along, and when about to give up and start north, he saw the print of a huge paw. Dropping from his white horse, he studied it and the other prints he could see. It was the track of a mountain lion, and it was heading right back into the lava!

Following on foot, Hopalong trailed the big cat back into a notch that finally seemed to end in a small clump of juniper. Pushing through it, Hopalong saw that here there was a space between the flows of lava that seemed to go deep inside. Returning, he built his cairn and then led Topper through the junipers after him. The track of the lion was steady along the narrow path, and knowing the nature of the big cat, Hopalong knew it was going to a den. There was no possibility of prey back in these wilds, and only a den or water would lead it into the wasteland. There was no evidence that any other living creature had ever advanced along this trail.

For a half hour he followed the trail, but then it suddenly began to slant steeply down and he saw the green tops of pines. In a hollow that barely had room for his horse to turn he picketed the animal; then, lying down, he wormed over the lava toward the treetops.

Below him lay a bowl-like depression no more than three acres in extent and walled around with pines. A few scattered trees through the center and, against the far wall, a half-ruined rock house. A stream of water trickled from a crack in the rock, a formation of limestone and sandstone around which the lava had flowed, leaving behind the walled-in space where the grass was rich and green, the trees tall. Five horses grazed nearby, and as he watched, Hopalong saw a man come from the rock house and throw out a pan of water. It was Dud Leeman.

Returning to the break in the flow across which he had come, Hopalong worked his way back up it until he arrived at the bowl he had seen from above. It ended among a jumble of rocks and a dense growth of manzanita and pine. He took a step forward and heard a low snarl of warning. Turning his head, he saw the mountain lion crouched on a rock above him and to his left. The cat was big. He could see only the head and shoulders, but they were sufficient to tell him that the cat was one of the largest he had ever seen. With its ears lying back, it stared at him from green, malignant eyes, then snarled, showing its fangs.

He stood flat-footed and stared at it. A mountain lion will rarely attack a man. Yet this one might consider himself cornered and, in such a case, would most certainly fight. A shot would warn Jacks, and then it would be a bitter fight for his life against three outlaws as well as the cat. He waited, his gun in his hand. The cat snarled again and seemed in doubt what to do. Hopalong stood perfectly still, giving the cat neither the invitation of retreat nor the fear of advance.

After a moment the cat rose from its crouch and then, after a long look, drew back and disappeared. Hopalong let go a heavy sigh of relief.

He worked his way through the trees within easy shooting distance of the house. He knew the range of his own gun and knew there wasn't a point in that three acres he could not cover, but he wanted to be close up.

Duck Bale came out of the house and walked directly toward him, then stooped to pick up an armful of wood. Some sixth sense must have warned him because he looked up.

"If you yell, Duck, I'll drill you!" Hopalong spoke softly.

Bale's flappy lips twisted. "Say, who—is it?"

"This is Cassidy—Red River Regan to you. Do like I say and you won't get hurt."

For an instant the outlaw stared at him, and then behind them a door slammed and a voice called out, "Duck! What's happened to you?"

From across the bowl a voice rang out: "Come out with your hands up, Dud! I want Jacks!"

Duck Bale hurled himself to one side and came up with a gun in his hand just as the bowl crashed and thundered with gunfire. Unseeing, Hopalong was staggering back. A shot from no-where had struck the tree beside him and splat-tered his face and eyes with fragments of bark. Hopalong shoved his gun back into his holster and rolled over on the ground, pawing at his stinging eyes, rolling to get under the brush and into some partial shelter. A shot kicked dust in his face, another ricocheted wildly off through the trees. Then he got his eyes opened and rolled behind a log. Suddenly there was no sound. Then the silence was broken by Bale's wild shout. "I got Cassidy! I killed Hopalong!"

"Shut up!" The voice was cold. "I slung that shot from the door!"

Hopalong felt a cold shiver of eagerness go over him. That was Jacks! He climbed slowly to his feet. From tree to tree he moved through the pines toward the clearing.

"How many were there?" That was Dud's voice.

"Two, I reckon. Well, with Cassidy down, the other one won't be so tough," Bale an-swered. "Let's get him."

"Wait." Clarry Jacks's voice sounded strange. "Maybe there are more."

"Only two shot," Dud said. "You sure you got Cassidy?"

"I saw him fall," Bale said. "He went down hard."

Lock, Cassidy realized, could probably hear all that was said. He would now believe Cassidy dead and would be working out some plan to handle all three of the outlaws. That he would never leave without a try at Clarry Jacks, Hopalong knew. As the bowl was small, whatever he did, Lock was sure to hear.

"Other one took out," Leeman said suddenly. "I'm havin' a look."

Belligerently, he started for the pines across the bowl. Hopalong saw Duck Bale stare uneasily after him, but Clarry Jacks turned abruptly and started toward the woods. Then he disappeared among the trees.

Hopalong waited, trying to locate Lock and to understand what the man had in mind. There was no sound from across the basin, but then, close at band, a twig cracked!

Silence, and then the sound of walking— not of creeping, but calm, easy walking, as if by a man out for a stroll, the sound of boots that stepped without fear, even with indifference.

Riveted, caught up by the spell of the moment, gripped in an iron band of suspense, he waited, watching an opening in the trees. There was something peculiar about the sound of those steps, something that did not seem quite natural.

"Cassidy!"

The voice was from behind him!

Hopalong's hands were poised, and the swing of his body threw the butt of his Colt into his hand. It leaped from the holster, the barrel lifting as he turned. Clarry Jacks, thin as a knife blade, his once-handsome face hard and vulpine now, stood at the edge of the woods. His draw was a blur of speed.

Hopalong's face was tight-drawn, like the face of a lynx, and from a half crouch his guns roared, stabbing daggers of flame that lanced across the shots of Clarry Jacks. Hopalong felt a bullet whiff hot breath past his ear, and with his guns roaring and bucking in his hands, he began to close in. Jacks stepped back, his shirt front a spreading crimson stain, his lips parted in a snarl that became a grimace.

Yet his guns lifted again, and Hopalong fired from both hands, seeing Jacks stagger as the heavy slugs smashed into his chest. The killer fell against a tree, blood filmed his face from a bullet wound in the head, and he fell, rolling over on one hand, the other clutching a gun.

Hopalong held his fire, waiting. The gun slipped from Jacks's fingers and the gunman slid to the ground, his nose plowing into the pine needles. Hopalong ran forward.

Dropping beside him, Hopalong turned the dying man on his back. Jacks's eyes flickered open. "Fooled—fooled you!" he whispered hoarsely. "Queer—echo." His eyes glazed over, and Hopalong got slowly to his feet, thumbing shells into his guns.

Ben Lock was coming along the path toward him, preceded by Duck Bale with his hands high. They were coming toward Hopalong, but the footsteps sounded behind him!

"What do you know?" Ben said wonderingly.

"It's the cliff back there," Bale said. "This whole basin has places like that all over it. It catches the sound somehow and makes it sound funny-like. Sounds seem to come from the wrong direction."

"Where's Dud?"

"He came into the woods after me," Ben replied. "He missed his first shot." Ben Lock looked down at the body of Clarry Jacks. "Well, you got him. Maybe Jesse will rest easy now."

.   .   .

They were within two miles of the Rocking R before Shorty sighted them. With Tex Milligan and Frenchy Ruyters they came racing down to meet the little cavalcade. Shorty looked at Bale.

"See you got the Duck," he said. "How about the others?"

"They won't bother anybody," Ben replied. He looked ahead to see Lenny Ronson racing a black mare from the ranch to meet them. "Better not tell her yet."

Hopalong drew up as Lenny swung alongside, and Ben rode on with his prisoner. Shorty Montana watched him go, grinning. "There goes an hombre who will be a married man inside the week! You wait and see!"

"He?" Milligan was surprised. "Who'll marry him?"

"Katie."

"Katie?" Frenchy stared. "I thought you had that claim staked. Wasn't that where you always hung out?"

"Sure it was." Montana grinned, his tough brown face lightening with good humor. "Katie's my sister!"

"Your sister?" Milligan stared at him in mock horror. "Who'd think a horny toad like you could come from the same basket as her! She's beautiful as a bay pony with three white feet, and you're as ugly as the mornin' after payday in a minin' town!"

"Huh!" Shorty sneered. "You should talk! You got a face like a lonesome jackass!"

Hopalong chuckled. It was time he was moving on to the 3 T L to look Gibson up. He'd gotten word that Red Connors would be there and Hopalong was looking forward to seeing his old friends again.

"Hoppy," Lenny suggested tentatively, "now the trouble is over we can have time to get acquainted. There's to be a dance and pie supper at the school Monday."

"Won't be able to make it." Hoppy smiled at Lenny, happiness bringing a strange radiance to his face. Lenny noticed it and looked at him in amazement.

"I was headed north," Hopalong continued, keeping his face grave, "and I better push on. Now with this fuss over, your brother won't need a fightin' segundo anymore."

He sighed deeply and cast a glance around, as if memorizing the distant mountains, the sparkling streams, the broad acres of rolling grasslands. "Sure like it here. But then," he added, "I'm a ridin' man. And I do get restless when things are quiet."

.   .   .

The morning sun found him on the edge of the Black Sand Desert. Hopalong eased the big guns on his thighs and looked between the horse's ears at the skyline. The wind was at his back and it carried a vague scent of pine down from the slopes of the mountains. It touched his collar and tugged at the brim of his hat.

Somewhere up ahead were towns where he had never been, country he had never seen. The trail stretched out before him, a thin line of possibilities worn in the sand. Hopalong Cassidy paused a moment, then urged Topper into a trot and pointed him at where the road crossed into the distance. His friends Red Connors and Mesquite Jenkins were waiting for him, and it had been a long time since he had seen Gibson of the 3 T L.

A Note of Explanation and Thanks

For those of you who have not read *The Rustlers of West Fork* and its Afterword, here is a brief history of my father's involvement with Hopalong Cassidy stories:

In the early 1950s, actor William Boyd took his version of the Cassidy character from the big screen to television. His earlier movies and Clarence Mulford's Hopalong books had been very popular and so Doubleday, Mulford's publisher, became interested in marketing some new Hoppy novels. Mulford, who had been retired since 1941, did not want to go back to the job and so he turned the task over to a young (actually not that young—Dad was 42) writer of pulp magazine westerns . . . Louis L'Amour.

The publishers chose the pen name Tex Burns for him and in 1950 and '51 he wrote his four Hopalong Cassidy books. They were published as the feature stories in the short-lived periodical, *Hopalong Cassidy's Western Magazine,* and in hardback by Doubleday. Due to a disagreement with the publisher over which interpretation of the Hopalong character to use (Dad wanted to use Mulford's original Hoppy, a red-haired, hard-drinking, foulmouthed, and rather bellicose cowhand, instead of Double-day's preference for the slick, heroic approach that Boyd adopted for his films) my father refused to admit that he had ever written those last four Hopalong stories. Starting with *The Rustlers of West Fork,* this is the first time that they have ever been published with his name on them. For a more in-depth version of the story of how Louis L'Amour came to write and then deny that he had written the Cassidy stories you can take a look at *Rustlers.*

In the same afterword I mentioned that, before he died, my father had wanted to include a note in the back of one of his books asking all of his readers to take it upon themselves to go out and plant a tree. So here I want to send out my special thanks to Ken Munro of Owen Sound, Ontario. He was the first reader to write and tell me that he had planted a tree, and he even sent along a picture of it. My father would have been very pleased.

Deforestation is not only a problem in the remote reaches of the Amazon, but right here in good old North America as well. Logging is one of the more destructive legacies left to us from the period of the Old West. We must replant forests in North America, even if it is only to supply the next generation with construction materials and paper products.

We must ask our legislators to limit cutting

and require replanting. Logging is a business that will not go away (nor should it, as a good portion of the population depends on it for a livelihood), but the industry, left to its own devices, would cut itself out of business. Like most American businesses based on natural resources, it knows little restraint, and would practice its craft until the last redwood toppled to the ground and the industry collapsed. If logging companies are forced to replant the trees they cut, with luck, there will still be a trade left for their grandchildren to practice.

We can also plant trees ourselves, as individuals. In the wilderness, in your yard (you might as well get pleasure from it), in a pot on your twentieth floor balcony. I urge you to do it anywhere you can and as often as you can. It is an inexpensive investment in our future.

To conclude, I want to offer my thanks to David R. Hastings II and Peter G. Hastings, Trustees of the Clarence E. Mulford Trust. Also to the late C. E. Mulford himself for creating the classic character of Hopalong Cassidy.

My best to you all.
Beau L'Amour

ABOUT LOUIS L'AMOUR

"I think of myself in the oral tradition—as a troubadour, a village taleteller, the man in the shadows of the campfire. That's the way I'd like to be remembered—as a storyteller. A good storyteller."

It is doubtful that any author could be as at home in the world recreated in his novels as Louis Dearborn L'Amour. Not only could he physically fill the boots of the rugged characters he wrote about, but he literally "walked the land my characters walk." His personal experiences as well as his lifelong devotion to historical research combined to give Mr. L'Amour the unique knowledge and understanding of people, events, and the challenge of the American frontier that became the hallmarks of his popularity.

Of French-Irish descent, Mr. L'Amour could trace his own family in North America back to the early 1600s and follow their steady progression westward, "always on the frontier." As a boy growing up in Jamestown, North Dakota, he absorbed all he could about his family's frontier heritage, including the story of his great-grandfather who was scalped by Sioux warriors.

Spurred by an eager curiosity and desire to

broaden his horizons, Mr. L'Amour left home at the age of fifteen and enjoyed a wide variety of jobs including seaman, lumberjack, elephant handler, skinner of dead cattle, assessment miner, and an officer in the tank destroyers during World War II. During his "yondering" days he also circled the world on a freighter, sailed a dhow on the Red Sea, was shipwrecked in the West Indies and stranded in the Mojave Desert. He won fifty-one of fifty-nine fights as a professional boxer and worked as a journalist and lecturer. He was a voracious reader and collector of rare books. His personal library contained 17,000 volumes.

Mr. L'Amour "wanted to write almost from the time I could talk." After developing a widespread following for his many frontier and adventure stories written for fiction magazines, Mr. L'Amour published his first full-length novel, *Hondo*, in the United States in 1953. Every one of his more than 100 books is in print; there are nearly 230 million copies of his books in print worldwide, making him one of the best-selling authors in modern literary history. His books have been translated into twenty languages, and more than forty-five of his novels and stories have been made into feature films and television movies.

His hardcover bestsellers include *The Lonesome Gods, The Walking Drum* (his twelfth-century historical novel), *Jubal Sackett, Last of the Breed,* and *The Haunted Mesa.* His memoir, *Education of a Wandering Man,* was a leading bestseller in 1989. Audio dramatizations and adaptations of many L'Amour stories are available on cassette tapes from Bantam Audio publishing.

The recipient of many great honors and awards, in 1983 Mr. L'Amour became the first novelist ever to be awarded the Congressional Gold Medal by the United States Congress in honor of his life's work. In 1984 he was also awarded the Medal of Freedom by President Reagan.

Louis L'Amour died on June 10, 1988. His wife, Kathy, and their two children, Beau and Angelique, carry the L'Amour tradition forward with new books written by the author during his lifetime to be published by Bantam well into the nineties—among them, two additional Hopalong Cassidy novels: *The Riders of High Rock,* and *Trouble Shooter*.